"The Fighting Wolf"

M/M Wolf Shifter Mpreg Paranormal Romance

The Cyan Conspiracy Vol 1

Apollo Surge

© 2021
Apollo Surge

This book is intended for Adults (ages 18+) only. The contents may be offensive to some readers. It may contain graphic language, explicit sexual content, and adult situations. May contain scenes of unprotected sex. Please do not read this book if you are offended by content as mentioned above or if you are under the age of 18. Please educate yourself on safe sex practices before making potentially life-changing decisions about sex in real life.

This story is a work of fiction. Names, characters, businesses, places, events and incidents are the products of the author's imagination or used in a fictitious manner and are not to be construed as real. Any resemblance to actual persons, living or dead, or actual events is purely coincidental. Products or brand names mentioned are trademarks of their respective holders or companies. The cover uses licensed images and are shown for illustrative purposes only. Any person(s) that may be depicted on the cover are simply models.

Edition v1.00 (2021.03.08)
apollo@apollosurge.com

Special thanks to the following volunteer readers who helped with proofreading: RB, Blue Savannah, Big Kidd and those who assisted but wished to be anonymous. Thank you so much for your support.

Chapter One

"ARE YOU READY?!" a man at the edge of the arena cried. There was a huge roar from all of those in attendance. The arena was a sand covered floor with a chain link cage running all around it. Bright lights beamed down into the arena, while the rest of the room was only dimly lit. The room stank of beer and sweat and blood. The baying crowd was hungry for raw, extreme action. They yelled and were so excited that they foamed at the mouth like beasts. Their eyes gleamed and they exchanged fistfuls of cash with the bookies to bet on their chosen warrior. Their faces were all broken and ashen. They had no strength to fight against the inexorable pressure of the world, so they came down into this hidden basement in this nameless city to watch people fight against each other for their amusement. This was nothing like the watered down, sanitized entertainment packaged and produced for TV audiences. It was not noble like the gladiatorial battles in the Colosseum, no, this was dirty and raw, passionate, it was two men using nothing but their fists to try and defeat the other, and it was glorious.

The air thrummed with excitement and anticipation. It was hot and grimy. Clothes clung to flesh, slick with sweat. This whole place was a taste for the forbidden.

There was one man in the cage so far: a huge man. He stood well over six feet tall and every inch of him was packed with muscle. There had likely never been a man who looked so mean. He had thick black hair that was tied back into a ponytail. His nose was crooked and jagged from where it had been broken before. His brow was stern and furrowed, his eyes dark and foreboding. His body glistened with sweat.

Drops trickled down the sculpted angles of his muscles, across dark patterns that had been etched into his skin. His mighty fists clenched and unclenched as he prepared for battle. He snarled and paced like a caged beast as he waited for his opponent. Looking at this man, it was impossible to think of anyone that could have beaten him. He was like a giant and he showed no sign of nerves whatsoever.

The man at the edge of the ring, a stocky man with a bald head and a wide smile on his face, for he was looking at all the cash being bet and thought about his cut, and what he'd buy with it. Oh yes, surely he would be able to afford a couple of beautiful, young women to shame themselves by spending the night with him, buying their virtue and their sins.

The cage door rattled as it opened and the opponent emerged from the shadows. In comparison with the giant this man was nothing. His body was lean and gaunt. There was some muscle definition, but it was more from hunger and malnourishment than because he had spent hours forging his body into a weapon like the giant had. His hair was short and his eyes darted about furtively. His skin was pale and there was a tremble to his hands. He staggered into the cage rather than striding. The noise deafened him. The lights blinded him. A lot of people laughed and started to increase their bets, eager to back the giant against this weakling.

Some of those who had a semblance of a conscience actually worried for the safety of this man, for they could see no other result than him being torn apart. Why was he here? Was he so desperate that he had been lured by the prize money if he survived, even though the risk was his life? Perhaps he had nothing left to live for. A lot of people in this grimy temple could understand that attitude. His shoulders were rounded and he licked his lips as he made his way into the middle of the arena. The giant looked him up and down and snarled again.

"Why are they sending me you? I wanted a challenge!" he roared. He spread his arms wide and turned to the crowd, basking in the glory before the duel had even begun. He nodded and smiled. "Looks like you'll all be getting home early tonight!" he cried. The crowd laughed.

But there were those who had seen this other man fight before. They knew what he was capable of, and they quietly smirked, confident that their money was safe.

The man at the edge of the arena yelled for the battle to begin. The giant turned and threw one of his mighty fists towards the smaller man. The fist was all sinew and thick knuckles. It hit with the force of a juggernaut. The smaller man's neck jerked and spit flew from his mouth as he was hurled to the ground by the impact of the blow. Bones rattled in his body and he felt the metallic taste of blood swim in his mouth. He groaned. The giant waved and bowed to the crowd, before turning back to the man on the floor. The giant towered over him. A huge shadow blocked the light. The giant straddled him. A huge weight pressed down on the middle of his body. A hand clamped around his head and the iron fist came crashing into his face again and again. Pain flared and sizzled and his head dropped, groggy. His vision was blurred. He cracked open his eyelids and looked up at the ceiling, at the bright light, the bright light that looked like the moon.

When he opened his mouth, he felt a warm river trickle out. Pain burst inside him, familiar pain. He breathed deeply. The roaring of the crowd seemed so far away.

"This was just a warmup!" the giant cried. "Next time I want someone who is worthy of me!"

He was acting as thought the fight was over. The smaller man knew it was far from over. There was still much to be done. He groaned as he pushed himself up. He spat out a thick glob of blood and it stained the floor. His knees trembled as he rose to his feet, and he stood again. A gasp rippled through the crowd. The giant noticed their change in attitude and turned. The snarl drifted away from his face as he saw his enemy rise. Shock and disbelief sat upon his face. Then the snarl returned. He strode forward and clasped the smaller man by the shoulders, driving his knee into the stomach. The smaller man felt the air rush out of him. He groaned and fell to his knees, heaving as he tried to catch his breath.

"Pathetic," the giant spat. The bookies ran through the crowd, trying to get the final bets before the fight was over, offering tempting odds as it seemed to be a sure thing. The smaller man looked up and past the giant, scanning the crowd. His gaze settled on a thin man, a well-dressed man with slick hair and an expensive watch, a man who didn't look as though he belonged in a place like this. The man gave one, long nod.

It was all the smaller man needed to know.

The giant roared as he kicked the smaller man. The smaller man quickly adjusted his hands to block the impact of the blow. The reverberations rippled up his arm in flaring pain and his body was sent flying across the ground, sweeping sand along with it. But then he rose on shaking limbs. Sand was pressed against his sweaty flesh. He embraced the pain and searched for the deep rage that burned inside him. The fire was incandescent and it was a release as it flowed through his blood. His skin was suddenly on fire and his eyes glowed. The taste of blood lingered on his tongue and he wanted more. His breathing grew deeper and his eyes focused. The crowd were chanting for blood, but as they saw what was happening, they gasped in disbelief. The giant saw too, and upon his face was a mixture of horror and disgust.

The only ones who were still smiling were the ones who were going to make a lot of money.

The body transformed. The flesh stretched and the bones grew. Thick, sharp claws protruded from paws. The thin, weak body turned into something powerful, something that was knotted with sinews and packed with muscle. Teeth sharpened into fangs. Ears grew. Fur started to appear. It was tempting to change more, to heed the call that was incessant in his mind, but he remembered his orders and he remembered the chain that had whipped him.

He could only go so far.

This was far enough.

He lunged forward towards the giant. The world had shifted around him. Now the smells were muskier and sharper. His vision was more intense. Everything seemed more...*alive*. He could taste the sweat in the air and he could taste something else as well, something that he always tasted on the people he fought: fear.

The giant wasn't sure what was happening, but he was a fighter, so he wasn't about to run. He lurched forward and aimed a right hook at the beast's face. The beast reacted quickly and caught his fist. The beast squeezed with all his might. The giant's roar turned into a shriek as his fist was crunched and he was forced to his knees. The beast kicked out with one of his powerful feet, sending the giant flying. He sprawled across the surface of the arena, his broken, withered hand trembling weakly. The beast cut the distance between them in no time at all and picked up the giant's body. The beast lifted it over his head, picking up this huge man as though he was nothing and then slammed him into the side of the cage. The chain links rattled and the whole arena seemed to shake. Sharp teeth glistened with saliva, with hunger. Everything seemed to fade away. There was a pulsing, throbbing feeling in the back of his head. There was something he was trying to remember…something important.

The giant was twitching on the ground. The beast slashed his back, leaving deep gashes. Blood oozed out of the torn flesh and it made the air sizzle. The beast knelt and was just about to give into his hunger when he heard a loud noise. The door opened again and a chunk of meat was thrown in, raw and thick. The smell was intoxicating and the beast was drawn towards it. He scampered across the arena using all four limbs and tore into the meat, tearing the tough steak apart. The taste sated him and brought him some peace. And then…then he felt his muscles weaken and his mind grow hazy. It was as though this was all just a dream. He looked up and he thought he saw the moon, but then he crashed into darkness.

***

"Alexander, this is your cut, wake up."

Alexander blinked and regained his senses. As soon as he realized he was awake he bolted upright and looked at his hands. The claws had returned inside him and he was left with fingers. His jaw ached. He touched the tender skin, but it would soon heal. He was perched on the edge of his bed. Before him stood the man in the suit, Richard. He held out a cluster of notes. His watch gleamed, as did the rings on his fingers. Alexander reached over for a glass of water. The liquid trembled in the glass as he brought it to his lips.

"Thank you," he said, taking the money. "Did he...is that man alright?"

"Of course he is," Richard said. "As well as anyone can be when they step into the ring with the beast, of course," he beamed. Alex shuddered inside at the reference to the beast. "You did well tonight. Despite your reputation people still wanted to bet against you, especially after you took that first punch. So many of them thought the fight was over then. You're such a special talent Alexander. In fact I think you might well be the best I've ever had. But I think we need to work on your discipline. You know you're not supposed to claw people."

Pain flashed in Alex's mind as he thought about the chain whipping him, training him to not let the bloodlust consume him.

"I won't let it happen again," he said in a small voice.

"See that it doesn't. That would lead to...complications. But don't feel too bad. You did very well for me and there are plenty of people who are eager to test themselves against you. There are so many of them who don't believe the tales of your prowess, so we're going to be making a lot more money. But for now you should get your rest." Richard patted Alex on the shoulder. Alex's shoulders were slumped. "Are you sure I can't get you anything? Any of the girls would be happy to come and keep you company."

Alex shook his head. Richard sighed and clasped his hands in front of his stomach. "I'll never understand you Alexander. These are the best years of your life; you should enjoy them!"

"Maybe one day," Alexander said. Richard chuckled to himself and left Alexander alone.

Alexander looked around at the small room he called home. There was a bedside cabinet beside his bed, and a small shelf on the other side of the room filled with books, all of which he had read. A closet was in another corner, which held his clothes, and at the end of the bed was the window. He crawled up to it and looked out at the murky night. The clouds were foreboding and gloomy. Behind them twinkling stars peeked out, but those were few and far between. The only thing that gave him some sense of solace was the moon. It was bright and beautiful, and it seemed to whisper to him, although he could not understand what it was saying.

One day, perhaps…one day he would understand. There were so many things he didn't understand. He stared at the moon for a while longer before he surrendered to bed and allowed his tormented dreams to come to his mind. The fight never ended for him.

Chapter Two

Ben stared in disbelief at what he had just witnessed. He was filled with a mixture of awe and disgust and shock. It seemed surreal, unreal even. He looked around and then pinched himself to make sure he was actually conscious, as it felt he was lost in an illusion. There were groans all around him as people wondered how the giant could have lost the fight. Bookies offered hollow apologies as they paid out the winnings to the people who had bet on the smaller man, the man whom Ben had been sure was going to be killed.

Suddenly panic started to set in. A lump formed in his throat and he was filled with the feeling that he had seen something he was not meant to see. People poured into the cage. Some of them dragged the giant away. The man was unconscious. Blood trickled down the gashes on his back and his hand was still clenched in a fist. The echo of the sickening crack of bone lingered in Bens' mind and nausea swirled in his stomach. Others bound the beast's arms and legs and chains and placed him on a stretcher. The...animal, for there was no better term to describe it, seemed to have been drugged by the steak it had eaten. Ben dreaded to think what would have happened had it not been sedated. He wasn't sure if the chain ring would have been able to hold the beast inside.

But what kind of beast was this? Ben still couldn't believe that he had seen a man shift like that. And the beast, it was like nothing Ben had ever seen before. His throat ran dry when he thought about it and all he wanted was to get out of there. He pushed his way through the throng of people and walked up the stairs, back to the main club. It was like stepping into another world. The main gentleman's club was a sleek place filled with a quiet ambience. Beautiful, scantily clad woman walked around, serving drinks, and displaying themselves. In a place like this everything was available for a price. The unspoken secret of the basement went ignored. Some people went up to the bar to drown their sorrows. Others spent their winnings on enjoying the women. Others, like Ben, made their way to the exit.

On the way, he was stopped by one waitress who gave him a sultry look.

"Don't leave just yet handsome, stay a while, the night is still young and there's plenty of time for magic," she said in a husky voice. Ben smirked.

"Believe me, we'd be wasting both our time," he said, glad that he was immune to the seductive charm of a place like this. He resisted the urge to sprint out of the door and walked at a slow place, not wanting to draw attention to himself. When he emerged the cool air of the night hit him and he walked down the street before turning into an alley, where he pressed his arms against the wall and breathed deeply, almost retching up the sandwich he'd eaten earlier. His mind was alive with wild speculation and his heart beat fiercely. He had only gone to figure out a story about the underground fight club, but now there was something else going on, something bigger. But where was he even going to begin?

He staggered home as the moon watched over him. Out here, the city was quiet, and it was a place where a man could feel truly alone. Images danced in the shadows, but Ben ignored all of them as he couldn't stop thinking about what he had seen. When he returned home, he stayed up thinking, thinking, and before he went to sleep, he sketched a drawing of the beast. When he looked at it his heart froze, and he honestly wasn't sure what to feel.

∗∗∗

His feelings hadn't changed by the morning either. After a rough night's sleep he rose and splashed cold water on his face. He looked in the mirror and wondered when he had lost the bloom of youth. Was it the job that made him jaded or was it just the state of the world? His mind turned back to the previous night and an unsettling feeling resided in the pit of his stomach. He walked back out into the front room of his small apartment and gazed at the sketch he had made. He picked it up and traced the lines with his finger. He had drawn the beast, but the beast had also been a man. What was his story? How had this happened to him? There were so many questions, and each one of them led to a dangerous place. The smart thing to do would have been to not ask them at all, to throw this drawing away and forget he had ever seen anything, but Ben couldn't do that. He was a journalist and he had to follow the story, no matter where it may lead.

For now, he had to follow the story back to where this had begun.

He grabbed some breakfast and walked outside. The morning was fresh and the sky was clear and blue. It was the kind of morning where it was easy to get lost in the beauty of the world and not even realize the horrors that lurked under the surface. As Ben made his way to the park in the middle of the city, he gazed surreptitiously at the people walking by, wondering if any of them were actually aware of all the horrible corruption that lay underneath the surface of civility. Perhaps they had their secrets. Everyone did. Everyone wore a mask. Everyone had a beast inside.

Ben shook the thought from his mind as he entered the park and walked through the wide, winding paths. The colorful flowers burst with a vivid energy and the trees rippled as a soft breeze ran through them. It was early morning and the park wasn't very busy. There were a few people walking their dogs, some were jogging, and others were just walking through the park on their way to work. Ben made his way to the lake. The boathouse wasn't yet open, so the boats were tied together near the shore, gently bobbing on the water. Benches were placed around the outside of the lake. The water looked glassy, and it glistened as the morning sun beamed upon it.

The vast majority of them were unoccupied, but Ben saw the man he had come to see. Alfie was sitting with a newspaper on his lap, gazing out at the lake. Ben walked up to him and Alfie shifted when he saw Ben approach.

"What do you want?" Alfie asked. "I told you everything I know. I don't want to be involved no more."

Alfie was in his thirties, about a decade older than Ben, but he looked much older than that. His nose was crooked, half of his right ear had been torn off, and there was a tremor in his left hand. His clothes were stained and tattered, and there was a musty smell that lingered around him. He was just one of the many people that life had been unkind to.

Ben wore a smug smile, projecting an air of confidence as he sat on the bench beside Alfie.

"Now I don't think that's quite true, is it Alfie?" Ben arched his eyebrow and let his gaze linger on Alfie. Alfie gulped and crossed his arms tightly.

"I don't know what you're talking about," Alfie muttered. Ben sighed and pulled out the drawing of the beast. Recognition and fear flickered in Alfie's eyes, and then he turned his head away. "Nice drawing," he said.

"I think you know what this is Alfie. I went there last night and this was one of the fighters. What's going on here?"

"Exactly what I told you was going on. I said I'd help you expose this fight club and that's what I've done. I did my part; whatever happens next is completely up to you."

"Oh no; you're not going to get off that easily. You never made any mention of this and I can't believe that this is something that would have slipped your attention. How could you not tell me about this?"

"How could I?" Alfie muttered after a few moments of silence. "Who would have believed me? If I had told you there was…this," he gestured to the drawing, "you would have dismissed me as some crank who had lost his mind. I thought it was better that you saw for yourself and maybe you can do something about it."

"Who is he? Where did he come from?"

"I don't know. I was never that close to Mr. Hammond. All I know is he was getting excited about a new fighter. Obviously when the kid arrived, I didn't think much of him and didn't see why Mr. Hammond was so excited. But then he started fighting and he…he changed. He was a beast. I think Mr. Hammond just saw dollar signs."

"But how does it work? How do they control him?"

"Training. And the kid is…" Alfie shook his head. "he just seems lost. That's the best way I can describe him, but obviously I never got to know him that well. I was already thinking of getting out and then when I saw what this kid could do…there was no way in hell I was getting in the arena with him. It was going further than I wanted it to. I don't know what Mr. Hammond was getting involved with. I don't know where he found this kid or how…this happened to him," again, he gestured at the picture. "All I knew is that I wanted out, and that someone should know about this."

"And that's where I come in."

"Exactly," Alfie said. "I don't want any other part in this. If Mr. Hammond should find out that I spoke to you I'm dead," he glanced around furtively and rose. "Can you imagine if there are more of them?" he hissed before he shuffled away. He walked with a limp and gasped in pain as he left Ben sitting on the bench. Ben shook his head in pity at Alfie's plight. He remained a while longer, before he left the lake and made his way to his office, troubled at where this story might lead.

Chapter Three

The night was stormy. Lightning crackled. There were screams in the background.

"Go," a voice whispered. All Alex remembered was that he didn't want to go. The ground was soft under his feet. The moon was high, surrounded by twinkling stars that peeked through the angry clouds. There were loud bangs and howls. He remembered the tender touch and that it must have meant something. It was warm on his cheek, so warm when everything else was cold.

The ground seemed to shake and Alex was afraid. He was pushed away by...by someone, but he didn't want to leave them. They told him to go, but he wanted to stay. They told him to run, but to where? Alex didn't know anyone else. Everything seemed so big. Even the trees were giant. The bushes rustled and others emerged wearing dark clothes. They shouted. Alex could hear the anger in their voices. He had been about to run, but then they grabbed her. Alex felt the fury inside, the ball of rage that expanded and exploded and burned with all the intensity of a bursting star. He had been told to run, but he knew he had to fight. He raced to try and save her but then something sharp crackled against him and he felt himself slumping to the ground. His body twitched and he saw shadows come over him.

"Do we take him? Even though he's a runt?"

"Sure, take them all. I'm sure they'll find something to do with him, and if not, he'll be food for the others."

The words were followed by a cackling laughter. Alex didn't understand. Who were these people? Why were they here? What was this memory?

It all faded into darkness and Alex was left grasping for meaning, searching for something that was elusive. He could feel that it was somewhere deep in his mind, but it was a whisper that ran away from him and disappeared, as though it had turned invisible.

And then there were chains.

***

Alex awoke in pain and anguish, as he often did. There was a tense pain in his stomach and a throbbing sensation behind his eyes. He wished he knew more, he wished he could sense more about his past and why he was here, who he was, but it was all such a blur. He swung his legs around and leaned on his knees, breathing deeply as he tried to calm himself. Outside the sun shone through the window. He thought of the battle last night. The pain had faded now. He had always healed quickly. Richard – Mr. Hammond, thought that it was wonderful. He always said that Alex was special, that he was very talented. Alex didn't know why though. It was just normal to him. He didn't do anything to control this.

Alex got dressed and walked downstairs. The club wasn't open at this hour. Cleaners were refreshing the bar after the previous night's activities. Mr. Hammond was sitting at a table, smoking a cigar while his wife, Andrea, stood by his side. She was much younger than Mr. Hammond and wore a pretty white dress. Her skin was porcelain and the sparkling jewelry made her seem as though she was like one of the rings that rest on Mr. Hammond's fingers.

"Good morning Alex!" Andrea squealed. She rushed up to Alex and hugged him tightly. The air around Alex was now heavy with the sweet, overwhelming scent of her perfume. He almost gagged. She pressed her body against him and smiled widely. "Richie told me what happened last night and I just wanted to thank you because the better you do the more jewelry Richie buys me," she beamed and fluttered her eyelashes. Alex smiled weakly and nodded.

"You're welcome," he said. There was so much he still didn't understand about this place, this world.

"Have a seat Alex," Richie said, gesturing to the seat opposite him. "Andrea darling, go and tell the kitchen to make up Alex a big breakfast. Give him the works. I bet he worked up an appetite after last night. A fighter always needs a big breakfast, you've got to keep that strength up," Richard said with twinkling eyes. He squeezed Andrea's hand and she scurried away like a faithful puppy. "She's a real sweetie, you know, I never thought I'd marry again but when I saw Andrea, well, a beautiful woman can make a fool of any man," Richie said. Alex smiled.

"Where did I come from?" Alex asked. Richie was in the middle of puffing on his cigar. He held the smoke in his mouth for a moment longer than he would have otherwise, and let it out in a long plume. He leaned forward and rested his arms on the edge of the table.

"Come on Alex, why are you so concerned about where you come from? None of that stuff matters in the world today. The past doesn't matter; the only thing that matters is where you end up. That's it. That's all. Where you are where you're going; that's what you have to be worried about."

Alex tilted his head. "Where am I going then?"

Richie grinned. "If you stick with me, I'll take you right to the top."

Alex wasn't sure what he meant by that, and he was still troubled.

"It's just...I have these dreams and I-"

"Dreams? What kind of dreams?"

Alex shrugged. "Just dreams."

"What are you doing in these dreams?"

"I'm...I'm in a forest I think and it's very loud. And there are people yelling at me telling me to go, but I don't go. And I keep thinking that there's more to these dreams, but I can never find it, and I feel that way about a lot of things. I always feel like there's something more...as though there's something I'm missing. But I'm not sure what it is or how to find it."

Richie sighed and leaned back in his chair. "It's just a dream Alex. You know, I'm an open minded guy, but all this talk about dreams meaning things has never really sat right with me. There have been a lot of people throughout the history of the world who have tried to give meanings to dreams, but when it comes down to it, it's probably just the brain sorting out all the information from the day. And you know there are some dreams that you don't even remember! So it's impossible to piece together everything. I'm sure it's nothing you have to worry about. Now, I know that it's difficult for you to feel like you don't know who you are, but that's why I'm here. You're a fighter Alex, you defy the odds and you defeat anyone who gets put in front of you. You're the best fighter I've ever known and you should be proud of that."

"I am. I'm glad I can be good at something, but I..." Alex trailed off. His gaze drifted to the empty stage and the silver pole that rose from the stage to the ceiling. He breathed deeply.

"Alexander, come on, you know what we've always said to each other; no secrets. I always want you to be honest with me even if it's something you're a little worried about telling me. Hiding things from people only ever leads to trouble. Believe me, that's what caused the end of my first marriage. I tried to keep my business and my personal life separate and it all blew up in my face. That's why things work out between Andrea and I, because she knows everything and I can trust her. Trust, it's the best thing in the world. I trust you with everything, and I want you to be able to trust me as well." Richard reached over and placed his hand on Alex's. "Alexander, you're like the son I never had," he smiled. Alex nodded and now he felt guilty at the thought of every lying to him.

"I...it's just that, well...I'm not sure that I enjoy fighting. I know I'm good at it, but hurting all these people...it feels wrong somehow." His gaze drifted down to his hands and he breathed deeply. Mr. Hammond pursed his lips and remained silent for a few moments. A lump formed in Alex's throat and his skin grew warm as he was afraid that Mr. Hammond was angry with him.

"Alexander, look, the truth about the world is that most people don't like their jobs. I had a lot of jobs I didn't like when I was your age, but I worked hard, kept my head down, and I managed to take advantage of opportunities that came my way to allow myself a certain freedom. You can do the same. It's not going to be a quick process, but it's something you can work towards. You don't have to enjoy a job, you just have to do it. And let's be honest, it's not like you're fighting people who can't take. All these men know what they're getting themselves in for and if it makes you feel better none of them are good people. The guy you fought last night for instance, do you know why he was fighting?" Alex shook his head. "He just got out of prison. He was inside because he caught his ex cheating on him and he broke her arm, but that was nothing compared to what he did with the guy she was cheating with. He actually ripped his dick off," Mr. Hammed winced as he said this, and broke his cigar in two as if to demonstrate. Alex furrowed his brow. "So you see, in a way you're doing the world a favor. I know it might not always seem like it, but just try not to let things get the better of you. It's okay to have these doubts and these worries, but don't let them ruin life for you. It's something to be enjoyed. You're in a wonderful city in the best country in the world, and you have everything at your fingertips, all you have to do is enjoy it," Mr. Hammond said just as Andrea returned, bringing with her a wide plate that was filled with food.

She placed it on the table and then Mr. Hammond rose. "Now Alexander, you go and enjoy your breakfast and I'm going to enjoy mine." He winked at Alex and then turned to Andrea, pinching her bottom. She giggled and slapped him playfully. He growled, and then chased her out of the room.

Alex sighed as he tucked into his breakfast. The food was delicious and it filled a hole in his stomach, but as he looked around the dim bar, he found himself unsatisfied by what Mr. Hammond had said. He was certain these dreams meant something, but what?

At that point he flinched as he heard chains rattle. The doors to the bar opened and a delivery was brought in. The boxes were fastened with chains, and they clinked as they were undone. Alex shuddered and nausea rose in his throat as he remembered what had happened when he had first come to Mr. Hammond. He didn't even remember how Mr. Hammond had found him. It was as though one moment he had just appeared out of nowhere. Alex had been confused. There were loud things, and lots of people, mean looking people who didn't seem to care about Alex at all. They tested him and fought him and pushed him until...until Alex's blood ran hot and the beast was unleashed and then...Alex clamped his eyes tightly shut...then the chains came, whipping against him, lashing his flesh, wrapping around his thighs and arms and ankles and wrists. He remembered the howls of pain that emerged from his own throat. He pulled back his sleeve and looked at the flawless flesh. The scars had healed, but even so he could remember the pain and how the metal bit into his flesh. They were always there, whenever he threatened to get too far, whenever he threatened to be too powerful.

But, Alex wondered, what would happen if he did go farther. He could hear the calling of the beast. There was something else waiting for him, something tempting him. Whenever his blood ran hot, he knew there was more, but the chains held him back.

What were they trying to stop?

Chapter Four

"You're late," William said sternly, peering over his horn-rimmed glasses. He was standing in the middle of the office with an article in his hand when Ben broke through the heavy double doors of *The White Flag*.

"I know, I'm sorry, but it's worth it when you hear what I have to say," Ben said. William huffed. He was a thin man with a narrow face and beady eyes that always seemed to be set in a withering stare. Ben thought he would have made a good headmaster. He smiled at the others in the office. William was currently standing next to Amelia's desk. He scanned the rest of her article, made a few slashes with his pen, and then handed it back to her.

"Re-write this and get it back to me. Remember that you're reporting the news, not writing a book. Our readers don't want these literary flourishes. They want the facts, nothing more, nothing less," he said. Amelia rolled her eyes as she swung her chair around and her hands fell back onto the keyboard. She arched her eyebrows at Ben, who offered her a withering smile. William snapped his fingers and strode back to his office. Ben fell into step and closed the door behind him.

"Okay, so what is this about then? Why are you late?" William asked.

"I had to speak to my source again, to confirm something about last night," Ben said. William leaned forward and arched an eyebrow. He could be a curmudgeon, but when it came to the news, he was often passionate. His desk was like the man, neat and orderly, with nothing out of place. On the wall were pictures of the things he treasured most; one was of a picture of him holding a huge fish he had caught, and the others were of his family. Whenever Ben was in this office, he was often struck by the thought of William having a family. He couldn't imagine William being in love or being tender, for he was so prickly and regimented in the office. And yet he had a family. It made Ben feel uneasy that a man like William could have a family while Ben was still searching for something special. He wasn't sure if it was envy or resentment, but there was something that seemed unfair. It all seemed so easy for other people...

"There's something to this story then?"

"More than I initially thought," Ben said. "I went to Hammond's club and managed to get downstairs. The fight club is this horrible place. They have a chain ring in the middle where the people fight, and as far as I can tell there's only one rule; the fight goes on until one of them is unable to continue. There's unregulated betting, there are people baying for blood. At times I thought I was in a slaughterhouse."

"Did you get an estimate of how much money was exchanging hands?"

"A lot," Ben said.

William rubbed his hands together and wore a predatory smile. "And I bet none of it is declared on his accounts. This could be it Ben, finally, we could get Hammond. An illegal fight club, undeclared profits, oh the IRS and the state are going to have a field day for this. Once this story comes out there's going to be nowhere for him to run; he's managed to slip away for so long, but now finally something is going to stick. I want you to write this up as quickly as possible."

"I will, but there's something else," Ben said. William looked at him expectantly, but Ben wasn't entirely sure what to say.

"Well?" William prompted. Ben licked his lips. Now that he was in this office far away from the grim basement fight club, everything he had seen in there seemed unreal. Was it possible that his mind had just been playing tricks on him? No…no…he had seen what he had seen and there was no denying that, even if it seemed impossible. Instead of saying anything, Ben decided to show William. He pulled out his sketch and placed it in front of him. William looked at it nonplussed.

"What am I looking at here? Is this your proposal for a new cartoon or something?"

"No, it's what I saw at the fight club last night. There was this one fighter, he was a beast."

"What, like an animal? I suppose we can get Hammond on animal cruelty as well. We might as well get him on as much as possible," William said stroking his chin.

"No, it wasn't an animal," Ben said. "It was…something else."

"Well, what was it?" William asked, a demanding tone creeping into his voice.

"I'm not sure exactly. That sketch is about the best that I can come up with. It was…it was the fighter. He started off as a man and then he changed into that," Ben pointed at the drawing that William was staring at. As Ben spoke, he realized how stupid he sounded and his voice faltered.

"What do you mean he changed?"

"I mean he changed, he transformed. I saw it with my own eyes. His body had this...I don't know, it was like a shimmering effect and then he grew. He became more muscular and his hands had these claws coming out of them. His body became covered in this hair and even his face changed; it looked longer than before and it...it's hard to describe, but it happened."

William put the drawing down and gazed directly at Ben, jabbing a finger towards him.

"Now look, I don't want any funny business ruining this story. I don't care what you do in your private time as long as it doesn't affect the work, but I'd suggest that you seek help for whatever drugs you're taking. This isn't normal and I'm not going to tolerate this kind of thing creeping into the stories. Are you trying to make a joke out of this? Are you trying to mock me?"

"N-no, not at all," Ben stammered, leaning into his chair as deeply as possible. William's words were harsh and stern.

"I don't know what you're playing at with this, but this has no place here at *The White Flag*. We're about truth, nothing more and nothing less."

"This is the truth. I saw it with my own eyes!" Ben protested.

William sighed and when he spoke again it was in a much calmer tone. "You may well have seen something like this. I don't know. I wasn't there. With everything that's been going on with technology it might well be the case that they used some kind of projection technology to add some flair to this fight club. But, frankly, it doesn't have any bearing on this story. If you write this people are going to dismiss it entirely. You know how it works. You might have the truest, most revealing exposé ever but if there's even one sentence that casts doubt upon it the whole piece is worthless. I've been after Hammond for most of my professional life and I'm not going to have anything jeopardizing that. This beast man or whatever it is isn't the story. The fight club is. The illegal gambling is. That is how we're going to take Hammond down. So this," he took the drawing and handed it back to Ben, "is not anything you need to concern yourself with. Is that clear?"

Ben nodded and pursed his lips. He rose from the desk, taking the drawing with him.

***

Ben worked diligently all day and wrote a good piece about the fight club. It was a piece that he could be proud of, but it wasn't the whole truth, so he felt unsatisfied with it. After he dashed off the final line, he emailed it to William, and then grabbed his satchel and strode out of the office, his mind clouded by everything that had happened. The drawing was in his satchel and he could almost feel it calling to him. It gnawed at him, because as much as he knew that it was important to take Hammond down with facts and nothing that could be dismissed easily, he also knew that there was a huge story here, something that might never have been reported on before.

As he strode out and waited for the elevator to take him down to the ground floor, he heard the patter of footsteps behind him and panting breaths calling him out. He looked behind him to see Amelia waving to him. Her red hair flowed out behind her like a fiery cape, and her cheeks were red.

"I think we could both use a drink, and a rant," she said. Ben nodded and they made their way to the bar down the street, which was their usual haunt whenever they needed to blow off steam after work.

***

"It just so frustrates me that he doesn't allow for any artistic expression. I'm not expecting to write any short stories or anything, but I hoped that I would be able to put my stamp on my stories. It's like he doesn't want any kind of individuality at all. He wants all the stories to be read in exactly the same way, as though the truth is enough to get people interested, but it's not. We need to have some way to engage people too. And I'm just so..." Amelia huffed and shook her head. She angrily peeled the label off her bottle of beer. "I never got into writing to be told that I shouldn't write well, or that I should dull my voice. If the job market weren't such crap, I'd honestly think about leaving because I don't feel like I can express myself. It feels like it's time for a change at the top."

Ben chuckled. "There's no way William is going to leave. He'll have to be dragged out, and even then, I think he'd find some way to cling on."

"Hence why I'm so frustrated. I know that nothing is going to change and I can't do anything about it. At least he actually likes you."

"I don't know about that."

"You're working on his pet project. He'd never let me anywhere near that. He'd be too afraid that I'd mess it up by injecting my own opinion," Amelia rolled her eyes and ran a hand through her thick hair, sweeping it behind her.

"Well, I don't think I'm doing it exactly the way he wants, and I'm having to hold certain things back."

"What things?" Amelia asked, the words rushing out of her quickly.

Ben sipped his drink and glanced around. Despite William telling him that he should keep certain things to himself, Ben knew he couldn't and especially not with Amelia.

"I saw something at the fight club last night, something very unusual. It's almost unbelievable, and I get why he doesn't want it to be part of the story because it makes it more likely that everyone is going to dismiss it, but it's also real, and I think it's worth following up on."

"What is it? What did you see?"

Ben leaned forward and lowered his voice to a whisper. "I know this is going to sound ridiculous, but there was a fighter there. He looked like just a regular guy. He wasn't overly tall or muscular and I had no idea what business he had in the arena. It looked as though it was going to be a slaughter at first, but then something happened. He...he changed."

"What do you mean 'changed'?" Amelia asked.

"He turned into this beast." Ben reached into his satchel and pulled out the drawing. "Into this."

Amelia took it and examined it. She arched her eyebrows. "What the hell is this?"

"That's exactly what I'm asking myself. I don't know. But I saw it with my own eyes. He changed and then he attacked the guy he was fighting, this giant of a man, as though it was nothing at all. He lifted him up...when I say giant, I mean this guy was a giant...and threw him."

"Wow."

"Yeah, it was...it was incredible really. I'd never seen anything like it. But he had this wild look in his eyes."

"What happened then? Did this beast just stop?"

Ben shook his head. "He slashed the back of the guy and there was a moment when I thought he was going to tear him apart. But then someone threw a steak into the arena. The beast went over, started to eat it, and then toppled over. It must have been drugged. It must be the only way to keep him under control."

"It sounds crazy. I can see why William didn't want you to write about it. I trust you more than anyone else in the world and I'm still wondering if you've gone insane."

Ben laughed dryly. "Oh yeah, you don't have to tell me that. I saw it myself and I'm wondering if I've lost my mind."

"It sounds...I don't even know how to describe it. Were you scared? It must have been quite an experience to see something like that."

"Hell yeah I was scared, but there was something else too." Ben thought back to the moment when he saw the mighty beast topple over, crumpling like paper. His limbs had sprawled across the arena and his tongue lolled out of his mouth. Then the handlers had all come in and dragged him away in restraints. Ben's heart sank. "It was actually quite sad."

"Sad?"

Ben nodded. "I mean, whatever has happened to him, he's still a person and he deserves to be treated better than this. He was just paraded out into this arena, forced to fight, and then drugged and dragged away. It was so unceremonious and pitiful."

"You really feel pity for this?" Amelia scrunched up her nose as she looked at the drawing, handing it back to Ben. He took it and stuffed it back in his satchel.

"You're only seeing the beast. I saw the man behind the beast. The more I think about him…he didn't really seem to be aware of what was going on. He looked lost and haunted. If he's being held captive something has to be done. It's not right for Hammond to get away with this. And what if this guy isn't the only one? I just don't know where to start looking, or where he could have come from."

Amelia looked uneasy. "You know that if you go after this William isn't going to be happy, and it's not going to be an easy story to write. Nobody is going to believe you, and I don't care where this all started; nobody is going to want to admit that they had a hand in it. But if you want to start somewhere maybe you should go back to Hammond's bar, try and see this guy for yourself. You're not really going to be able to do much unless you talk with him."

"I guess," Ben said.

"If he is a person as well as a beast then he's going to have to do the things normal people do, like go for walks. But there's something else as well. You ask who could have done something like this. What about Cyan?"

"Cyan?" Ben arched an eyebrow and sighed. He opened his hands and drummed his fingers against the table.

"You don't have to look at me like that. I know that with me everything comes back to Cyan, but this time it's legitimate! You remember a few years ago it was revealed they were doing illegal testing on animals, what if this has something to do with it?"

"What are you talking about?"

"I don't know, maybe they were trying to splice animal DNA into humans or something and this beast of yours is the result."

"I think you're getting into the realms of fantasy now," Ben said. "And they were cleared of all charges."

"Oh of course, the big mighty corporation that can afford all the best lawyers gets cleared of charges. Come on Ben, I thought you were smarter than that. The fact that they were declared innocent doesn't mean they are innocent, it just means they can afford to bribe those who makes the decision. All I'm saying is that if this isn't an aberration of nature then someone has to be behind this, and who likes to play god? Cyan."

Ben listened to what she was saying and despite his desires he couldn't dismiss her entirely. She had as much of a chip on her shoulder about Cyan as William did about Hammond. Neither of them seemed to be familiar with Moby Dick and how obsession can consume a person, but Ben couldn't deny that Cyan had been involved in some shady deals, and while he wasn't a conspiracy theorist it would have taken a lot of resources to create something like this beast, and there was nobody who had as many resources as Cyan.

"I'll do you a favor and look into this for you. It won't have to have anything to do with the story you're writing for William. We'll find out as much as we can and then take it to him, if we ever find out what's really going on here. You just go and try and talk to this guy. Who knows, maybe you'll just meet him and he'll tell you everything you need to know."

"Is our job ever that easy?" Ben asked with a smirk. Amelia threw back her head and laughed before she ordered another beer, but Ben declined to join her and slunk out into the night, making his way towards Hammond's bar. As he left, he looked towards the horizon and the towering skyscraper that rose higher than any other building in the city. At its peak was the blue triangle, the logo of the Cyan Corporation. The tower loomed over the city, engulfing everything in its shadow. Sometimes it seemed as though the city was a festering pit of corruption and at the heart of it was Cyan, but although many lawsuits had been brought against it over the years, nothing had stuck. It was impervious to assault and continued its operations. Was it possible that this corporation had its hand in this beast? If so, then why would they let it leave, and why would Hammond be able to get his hands on it? There were so many missing pieces to the jigsaw that Ben didn't even know what picture he was trying to make yet, but he was off to find another piece, and hoped that it would shed a little more light on the situation.

Chapter Five

The day had been long. Alex had stayed in the bar for a little while after his talk with Mr. Hammond, but then had returned to his room where he gazed out of the window. Mr. Hammond had advised him to not go out into the city because it was dangerous, both for him and for others. While Alex had a lot of control of his transformation, he was wary about losing it outside. It was one thing to fight in the pit, but if he would ever lose control outside then it could be deadly to anyone near him, and he wasn't sure when he would stop if Mr. Hammond wasn't there to bring him to a standstill. It was easier for everyone if he stayed in his room.

Besides, Alex didn't like the outside. It was big and open and it seemed as though anything could happen. It was safe in the small room with its four sturdy walls, a barrier he could count on to keep himself safe.

When the evening drew in, Alex ventured downstairs and skirted the room, taking not of the bubbling atmosphere. There were plenty of regulars that were already enjoying themselves. The waitresses were laughing and wrapping their arms around these men, men they held no affection for, and yet they acted just as Andrea did when she was around Mr. Hammond. It was a strange emotion and Alex didn't understand it at all. It was as though everyone here was playing a part. They knew they were playing a part, and yet they acted as though everything was real.

Many of the waitresses winked and smiled at Alex. A lot of them had offered him a taste of what he was missing. Alex wasn't entirely sure what that was, but he knew he didn't want what they were offering.

Other men seemed to be intoxicated by them, as though they were under a spell, but Alex didn't experience the same thing. It was just another way for him to feel like an outsider, or that there was something wrong with him.

Thankfully there wasn't a fight tonight. Mr. Hammond only opened the fighting arena on special occasions to make the allure more potent. He said that if it were common it would lose its appeal, and Alex would lose his mystery. Alex didn't mind. It meant that he was able to focus on doing other things. As he looked at the various people in the bar he wondered if any of them were struggling with the same problems he was struggling with. Did any of them have missing parts of their lives? Did any of them know who they truly were?

There were nights when he would stay in his room locked inside with his own thoughts, but recently he had enjoyed it more when he had been out in the crowd. The noise and the company helped to distract him. It had been overwhelming at first, but he was getting more used to it. He parked himself at the bar and Toby, the bartender, nodded at him and provided him with a Coke. Mr. Hammond said that Alex shouldn't drink because it was the way to the devil. Alex didn't mind as most of the drinks didn't smell nice anywhere, although nobody else seemed to be able to tell.

"Evening Alex, are you staying down here again tonight?" Emma asked. Alex knew it was her even before she leaned against the bar beside him, for he could sense her lavender aroma lingering in the air. Her black hair was tied in a long ponytail and she wore make up around her eyes, accentuating the almond shape. She had a soft voice and olive skin, and her eyes sparkled. Alex always felt self-conscious when he was in the arena clad only in a thin cloth around his waist, but Emma seemed perfectly comfortable even though most of her skin was exposed.

"Yes," Alex replied.

"I'm glad, it's always nice to know you're watching over us. Mr. Hammond said that you wouldn't let anything happen to us."

"I won't," Alex said.

"We're all very thankful for that. You know, there is a lot here that you could enjoy if you wanted to relax a little. I'd be happy to take you for a little dance, free of charge. Any friend of Mr. Hammond's is a friend of mine after all."

"I appreciate it Emma, but I'm okay here," Alex said.

Emma furrowed her brow and then laughed, slapping him playfully on the arm. "Oh you are a funny one Alex. You know that us and the rest of the girls have a bet going; the first one to make you crack wins. But you're...well...you're just different to the other men aren't you."

"Is that a bad thing?"

"No, not at all, but it does make me wonder what you really want out of life."

Alex curled his fingers around the glass. The condensation trickled down the side. Ice cubes bobbed in the fizzy liquid. He brought it to his mouth and let the sweetness slip between his lips.

"I don't know. I don't even know who I am really."

"Oh we've all been there," Emma said. She twisted her body so that she leaned her elbows against the bar and looked out onto the bar. "When I was younger, I had no idea what I wanted to be. Everyone expects you to figure it all out, and everyone else always seems to have it figured out, so you feel left behind. And when you don't figure it out, you end up in places like this," she smirked, but Alex noticed that there was no humor in her eyes.

"Do you not want to be here?"

"It's not that it's just…I always thought I was meant for something more, you know? I wanted to be a great actress lightning up the silver screen, but sometimes you make choices in life and you end up sealing your fate and there's no escaping it. But then you find other ways to escape it, new fates," she smiled.

"How do you go about doing something like that?" Alex asked.

"Well, that depends on what you want out of life. For me it was through other people, my kid, specifically. Sometimes if you don't know who you are you have to look to someone else to help you figure it out. Nathalie helped me figure it out. When she was born, I knew I had to be strong for her, and I knew that I had to be better than I was before. She's only a tiny little thing, but without her I know I wouldn't be the person I am." Emma's head dropped and a single tear trickled down her cheeks. She chuckled at herself a little and wiped the tear from her eye.

"I should get back to work. This look isn't going to be good for business," she said. "But don't worry about it, you're still young and you still have time to figure all this stuff out. But sometimes the only way you can be anyone in this world is to mean the world to someone else."

The words stayed with Alex as she walked away. She forced the sadness from her face and wore her practiced smile as she settled on the lap of a man who seemed overjoyed to see her even though they had never met before. Alex watched for a little while, and then turned away from this dance. His attention was caught by movement from the door. Mr. Hammond was standing there gesticulating wildly at a man who was unfamiliar to Alex. He was evidently not one of Mr. Hammond's regular associates.

When Alex saw this man his breath was taken away. Without thinking, he moved away from the bar and left his drink behind. Breath caught in his throat and his heart beat a little more quickly than usual. A haze drifted over his mind. It wasn't anything he remembered having experience before, but it was wonderful. It was as though bubbles rose through his body and made him lighter than air. The man looked slightly older than him, he was tall, with a kind face and a tousled mop of light brown hair. His lips were soft and full, and there were shadows under his eyes. He wore a creased shirt and he was reaching out to Mr. Hammond, who held a satchel.

"- and I don't need your kind sticking their nose into my establishment. This is private property and I don't need to let you in. You can tell your editor to go and shove his questions where the sun don't shine, and if he wants to come down here himself, he can rather than hide behind one of his lackeys. I don't care which paper you work for, but you don't have any business being here." Hammond thundered. Then he noticed that Alex was there. "Oh, Alexander, good. Here, look through this and make sure there's nothing suspicious. I don't trust this man. If there's a camera take it away and we'll destroy the film."

The satchel was shoved into Alex's chest. He gaped as he was thrust into this situation. The man's expression changed when he saw Alex. Their eyes met and it was as though Alex had been struck by a lightning bolt.

"Come on!" Mr. Hammond yelled. Alex could feel the weight of the stranger's gaze upon him. It made his cheeks burn and his stomach churn, but the feelings weren't entirely unwelcome. He rummaged through the satchel and came across a drawing. A drawing of him. Alex's hand trembled and he swallowed a lump in his throat as he glanced up at the stranger. There was an imploring look in his eyes, as if he were trying to tell Alex something, but Alex wasn't sure what. But this drawing, what did it mean? Did he know something about Alex?

Alex thrust the satchel back towards the stranger.

"There's nothing there," Alex said. Mr. Hammond smirked and walked away, shaking his head. The stranger stepped out of the bar and Alex was tempted to follow, but Mr. Hammond was already beckoning him over.

"Who was that?" Alex asked.

Mr. Hammond sighed as he placed his arm around Alex's shoulder. "That was someone who doesn't know how to mind his own business. You see Alex there are a lot of people in this world who like to interfere with the way other people choose to live their lives. Now, you see all this around you?" he gestured to the bar. "A lot of people would tell you this is wrong, but it's not. I provide a place for gentlemen of a certain class to have a good time, and should I be punished for that? No, I shouldn't, but some people have made it their life's mission to try and besmirch my reputation even though I'm only trying to make an honest living. Don't worry though, it's nothing for you to worry about. But I want you to be careful. If people come around here and ask questions, just tell them you don't know anything. It's why it's best that you say in this bar. It's safe for you in here. Nobody is going to try to take advantage of you. There are lots of games being played in this city and it's easy to lose if you don't know what you're doing, but don't worry, I'll teach you everything you need to know. You stick with me kid, and I'll make sure nothing steers you wrong."

"Yes Mr. Hammond," Alex said, although he gazed anxiously towards the door. He made an excuse that he was tired and had had enough of the bar for the night and then made his way back upstairs. He went into his room and then pried the window open. There was a small roof just beneath his window, and then an alley below that. He climbed out and jumped down, landing with a thud. His palms stung as he used them to lessen the impact of his landing, and then he was off. There was something about this stranger that had intrigued him and he wasn't ready to just let him leave. So much of Alex's life had been kept under wraps in Mr. Hammond's building, but if this stranger knew something about Alex then Alex owed it to himself to find out what that was.

He skulked along the sidewalk and sniffed the air, catching the scent of the stranger. It wasn't difficult as it had led an indelible mark on Alex's heart. He glanced in both directions and then followed the scent, being careful to stick to the walls as he felt safer. At one point a car rushed by, its engine roaring as loud as a hurricane, and Alex jumped. He swallowed his fear and continued to glance behind him, taking note of where he was going so that he wouldn't get lost on the way back home.

Being out and free like this unsettled him as it wasn't something that he was usually allowed to do. Mr. Hammond had always told him that the world was not a nice place and would only prove dangerous for someone like him. He said that if they ever saw him change that would treat him like a monster and take him away from Mr. Hammond. Alex didn't want that. He didn't want to go anywhere else. Somewhere deep inside him he knew that being taken away from home was the worst thing in the world, although he didn't know where he had learned that.

He followed the scent around a few corners and then saw the stranger ahead of him. Alex stopped for a moment, unsure of what to say, but then the stranger spoke, taking Alex by surprise.

Chapter Six

Amelia's idea to go and speak to Mr. Hammond had been dead on arrival. As soon as Ben had started asking questions Mr. Hammond had shut him down and told him to leave. He must have had some sixth sense about reporters coming to him. Ben hadn't even told him he worked for *The White Flag*, which suggested that Mr. Hammond had some rivalries with editors other than William. It had seemed like his efforts were futile, until Ben had seen him. Alexander had appeared from nowhere, like a bolt from the blue. Their eyes had locked and Ben had been utterly stunned by his appearance. He looked so...so normal, although there was a haunting quality to his eyes. Ben's heart had been in his mouth while Alexander had been searching his satchel. He must have seen the drawing, there was no doubt about that in Ben's mind. But Ben had been certain that he would show Mr. Hammond, and if so, that would have ended things right then and there. If Hammond had known Ben was looking for information about the beast, he would never have been able to leave.

But Alex had kept the secret.

Why?

There was more going on here and Ben knew that he couldn't just let this go. The intrigue was too tantalizing. He turned away from Hammond's establishment with his mind whirring, only to realize shortly after that he was being followed.

***

There was a shadow behind him. Ben twisted around the streets in an unfamiliar pattern, but still the shadow persisted. Whoever they were, they weren't good. Ben assumed that Hammond would have employed people who had better skills. He took a deep breath and tensed his muscles. He glanced around. The street was empty, meaning whoever was following him was likely to make his move. Ben would either fight or run, depending on how many people Hammond had sent after him. Most likely he would run. He couldn't imagine Hammond sending anyone other than a vicious, muscle-bound warrior, but it also told Ben that he was onto something. If Hammond was this troubled, then he was hiding something.

"Why are you following me?" he asked, directing his voice towards the shadows. He turned swallowing the fear that became a lump in his throat, and was shocked to see *him* standing there, the man that Hammond had called Alexander. There was a moment where they stood and stared at each other. Like in Hammond's bar it felt as though there was some kind of energy between them. A tingling sensation crawled over Ben's skin, as though a web of electricity settled over him. He tilted his head, and then Alex backed away.

"Wait," Ben said, holding out his hand. "I'm not going to hurt you."

"The...the drawing," Alex asked. "You had a drawing. Of me."

"Yes, of you," Ben said. He licked his lips as his heart beat frantically inside. He was so close he could feel it. He prayed that nothing would mess this up. "Who are you? How can you do this?"

"I'm Alex," he said, but offered nothing else. It was strange to see the man like this. He looked so pitiful, so lost and haunted. His skin was pale, his eyes wide. His hair was thick and dark. The look of innocence on his face belied the thing inside him. Ben was filled with a mixture of fear and intrigue. He stepped forward tentatively, not wanting to do anything to provoke Alex into changing, and yet also unable to drag himself away. Alex's gaze fell to the ground and he looked around, uncertain and uneasy.

"Where did you get the drawing?" he asked.

"I drew it myself. I was there, in the arena last night. I saw it all," Ben replied.

"Oh. I thought…you don't know anything else about me then? I thought maybe it was from before."

"Before when?"

"Before I was with Hammond."

"And how long have you been with him?"

Alex licked his lips and clasped his hands in front of his stomach. He shifted his weight between his feet. The illumination from the streetlight nearby cast half his face in shadow.

"Mr. Hammond told me I shouldn't answer your questions."

Ben paused before he spoke again, knowing that he would have to play this carefully if he was to keep Alex around without scaring him off.

"I don't care about Hammond," Ben lied. "It's just that I've never seen anyone like you before and I can't help wondering about how you can do what you do and where you came from. I'd just like to talk for a little while, if that's alright?" Alex glanced back towards the way they had come. "I know a quiet place where nobody will find us," Ben said, and he told Alex his name.

***

Alex nodded and Ben led him away, back to the park by the lake. It was still and silent. Halos of light spread under streetlights, while darkness and shadows lingered all around them. The twinkling lights of the city were visible at a raised glance and beyond them was the moon, hiding behind a veil of clouds. Alex led Ben to a bench and gestured for him to sit down.

"So how do you change?" Ben asked.

"It's just a part of me. I don't know how it happens really. There's a voice inside me, this feeling that calls to me, and I…I listen. And then I change."

"Does it hurt?"

"Sometimes. But I got used to it."

"Have you always been able to do this?"

Alex bit his lower lip and his leg started to jerk.

"I'm sorry," Ben continued. "I don't mean to ask you so many questions like this. I'm just honestly fascinated by it. I've never seen anything like it before. I get the impression that you don't talk about it much?"

"Mr. Hammond doesn't like me talking about it and I…I don't know what else to say. It's just something that I can do. I don't know why nobody else can't."

"Does Mr. Hammond not know?"

Alex shook his head.

"Do you not remember anything then? Where you came from? Your childhood? Your parents?" Ben asked.

Alex shook his head again. "I remember my name. I remember how to do things. I know about the world, but there are some things I don't know. Things about myself. I don't know who I really am. And I have these dreams..."

"Dreams?" Ben asked, his ears pricking up.

"They're just dreams. Mr. Hammond says I shouldn't pay any attention to them."

"How did Hammond find you?" Ben asked.

"I...I don't know. I just know that I was with him and he was telling me that I was going to be good for him, and that he would make me a star. He told me I was special. He takes care of me. He gives me a place to live."

"Yeah, but that's not giving you a life. I can see how nervous you are. Are you even supposed to be out here?"

"Mr. Hammond says that I shouldn't be out here in case anyone sees me. I don't want to be out here either. I'm afraid of what might happen. I'm afraid that I'll hurt someone."

Ben was amazed to hear him say this. "That's quite a strange thing to say from someone who fights in that arena. Do you like fighting?"

"It's just something I do. Mr. Hammond says I'm a natural."

"Do you enjoy it?"

Alex shrugged as he gazed across the lake. "It's just something I do."

"But what would happen if you didn't want to do it? Did Mr. Hammond even give you a choice?"

An uneasy looked flickered across Alex's face.

"No, he didn't."

Ben frowned. He leaned forward and his mind was alive with worry. Something about this definitely didn't seem right and his heart went out to this poor guy who was trapped. It was starting to sound like this was a bigger story than he had first imagined.

"You know that's not right, don't you Alex? You should never be forced into doing something that you don't want to do," Ben said. There was a look on Alex's face that didn't quite seem to understand, as though these things had never been explained to him before. Ben's heart burned with anger as he thought about Hammond and all the illegal pies he had his fingers in, and this seemed to be the worst of all. How could anyone bring themselves to take advantage of someone like Alex?

"I don't mind doing it. Mr. Hammond says that these are bad men."

Ben nodded. He wasn't about to tell Alex that he was wrong just yet.

"What do you think would happen if you told Mr. Hammond that you didn't want to fight any longer? What would he do if you said that you wanted to stop completely?"

"I don't know," Alex said in a hollow voice. His eyes suddenly darted up and his hands wrung more tightly together. "But I should go. If I'm gone too long Mr. Hammond will be angry." He rose abruptly, taking Ben by surprise. Alex started to stride away. Ben ran behind him, catching his arm and pulling him back.

"I know that we've only just met and I don't know you that well, but you must be going through a lot. I can't imagine what it's like not knowing who you are or why you can do what you can do. I get that there are a lot of things you don't understand about the world, but one thing you need to know is that friends help each other. If Hammond were your friend, surely he would try to help you figure out what's going on here, right?"

Alex looked at him blankly. Quickly, Ben pulled out a card and thrust it into Alex's palm. As their flesh touched his skin burned with a yearning feeling. "If you ever need to talk you can come and find me, okay?" Ben said. Alex stared at the card and then disappeared into the night, leaving Ben standing there, utterly perplexed. There was such a mystery surrounding this man, and such a pitiable fate as well. Ben couldn't imagine the torture of not knowing your own past, but it begged the question of why Hammond wouldn't allow Alex to discover it for himself? Was there more at play here? As Ben walked home, he glanced up at the towering Cyan building, wondering if Amelia was right and that their hands were all over this.

Chapter Seven

The following morning Alex awoke with a troubled mind. He had returned to the bar with no complications; as far as he could tell nobody had noticed he was gone. It didn't stop the guilt from burning in his heart though. He had gone directly against Mr. Hammond's orders, and Mr. Hammond was the only person he could trust.

At least that's what he had always believed.

He looked down at the card that he had placed under his pillow. Mr. Hammond had told him not to talk to a man like Ben, and yet Ben had been nothing but kind and concerned, and despite how difficult it was to listen to what he said, Alex couldn't ignore the fact that there were some aspects of his relationship with Mr. Hammond that were troubling. Whenever Alex brought up his past Mr. Hammond always said that it didn't matter, but it *did* matter. And he dreaded to think what would happen if he told Mr. Hammond directly that he didn't want to fight. Ben had voiced a question that Alex had barely dared to ask himself. He flinched as he thought about the chains and shuddered at the memories of pain that flashed through him.

He closed his hand around the card and thought about that moment where he had touched Ben's hand. It was the first kind of contact he'd had with a man that didn't involve anything violent and it was *nice*. Being around Ben made him feel funny inside; it was almost as though he was scared, and yet there was nothing to be scared of because Ben didn't pose a threat to him. The feelings were confusing and he rubbed his head, wishing that things weren't so difficult. They seemed so easy for everyone else. Why did life make sense to everyone else? Why didn't they have difficult questions to ask?

He placed the card in his bedside table and shut the drawer, deciding that for now it was better for him to not contact Ben. It would only anger Mr. Hammond.

***

When Alex ventured into the bar, he was nervous in case anyone had noticed him leaving the previous night. His anxiety increased when Mr. Hammond called him into a meeting. But as Alex walked into the room, Mr. Hammond smiled and greeted him with a warm hug. He seemed to be in a good mood and puffed happily on a cigar.

"What a beautiful day it is today," Mr. Hammond began, gesturing for Alex to sit down. The room was one that Mr. Hammond used for all his special, secret meetings. It was a small room, with a desk at one end and a then a circular table covered in green felt. There were six chairs placed around it. The room smelled heavy and musty, and it made Alex's stomach turn.

"Now I know you weren't expecting to fight for a few more weeks, but I had a very interesting proposal last night. It seems that someone has been keeping an eye on you and they want to test you against the very best. It's no doubt going to be the hardest fight you've ever had, but it's also going to be the most lucrative. Oh yes, it's another stepping stone on your rise. You're going to conquer the world, and I'll be right there by your side." Mr. Hammond strode around the office and stopped behind Alex. He placed his hands on Alex's shoulders and squeezed tightly.

"It's all coming together Alex. Our plan is finally coming to fruition. I know it's been frustrating to wait this long, but soon enough you'll have all the attention you can handle. People are going to want to see you fight all over the world. In China, Japan, New Zealand, the Middle East. There are lots of people who are going to pay us a lot of money just to see if the rumors are true, and you'll surprise them all. I'm so proud of you Alex." There was genuine emotion in his voice, but Alex closed his eyes and tried to stifle his own misgivings. He remembered what Ben had said about having a choice. Mr. Hammond had planned all of this out without ever asking him what he thought about it or if this is what he wanted. While the thought of journeying around the world was intriguing, Alex didn't like the idea of fighting over and over again. Every time he stepped into the arena it felt as though he lost a little part of himself, and he wondered how many fights it would take before his soul was condemned to hell, if it hadn't happened already.

"I'm not sure I want to," Alex said in a small voice.

Mr. Hammond suddenly went silent. The room filled with tension. His hands slipped away from Alex's shoulders. Thick smoke rose from his cigar. The smell almost made Alex choke.

"What do you mean?"

"I mean the fighting. I'm not sure it's what I want anymore. All these fights are too much."

"Too much?!" Mr. Hammond thundered. "What on earth are you talking about lad? You're a fighter. You've been bred for combat. It's your destiny. Where is all this coming from?" He spat in derision. "Is this to do with what you were saying before about how you're worried you're hurting people?" Mr. Hammond rolled his eyes. "Believe me, everyone knows what they're getting in for and fighting is a noble art. It's had a place in every society since people started gathering in tribes. You're a gladiator and you should be damned proud that people want to pay you good money to see you in action. A lot of people go through their lives forgotten and ignored. They spend their time on this planet wasting every opportunity they get and by the time they leave they've had no impact at all, and nobody remembers them. But you...yes...people remember you. What's more, they remember where they were when they first saw you. You provide them with a sense of awe and wonder and that's something that is almost invaluable. You should be proud of what you do Alex because there are few people who can conjure that kind of feeling in people."

Alex listened to the energetic vigor in his words, yet something still didn't seem right. Why did he have to fight to make that feeling happen?

Mr. Hammond strode around the table and leaned on the back of a chair, looking down upon Alex.

"Come on lad, this is good news! I thought you would have been happy. What's troubling you? You've never shown this kind of doubt before. This is what I brought you here for. This is the role you have to play."

"But why?" Alex asked.

"What do you mean why?"

"Why is this my role? Why isn't it something else? Why do I have to do this? Why can't I make the choice for myself?"

Mr. Hammond's features changed. The humor fell from his face and his voice turned to gravel.

"You did choose this Alex. You don't remember, do you?"

"Remember what?" Alex asked.

"The first time we met. You have no idea. The first thing you did was fight. That's all you've ever known. You've fought and you've bled and then you've fought some more. That thing you change into when you're fighting, that's the real you. This," he gestured lazily with one wave of the hand, "this is just a mask."

Alex felt as though he had been punched in the gut.

"But where did I come from? Where did you find me?" Alex asked, holding back a sob.

Mr. Hammond slammed his hands down on the table and glared at Alex. Alex could see the red rivers in his eyes and the yellow shade of his teeth. "I've told you before that what happened before doesn't matter. Whatever happened in your life before I found you doesn't matter. You belong to me, and you'll do what I say because I know best. This is the order of things and you would do well to listen to me, otherwise I'll cast you outside and leave to your own devices and let me tell you that the world is not kind to people it thinks are different. You wouldn't last a day out there without me. I take care of you, I protect you. All I ask in return is that you trust me. Alex, I know what's best for you. Just believe me when I say that and stop asking me about what happened before because it just doesn't matter. Think about the future. Life is about where you're going, not where you've been."

The outburst was passionate and the hot air rushed toward Alex. Mr. Hammond stormed out of the room, not giving Alex any chance to respond. Alex searched his mind, trying to find the memory of being found by Mr. Hammond, but no amount of searching turned it up. There were vague whispers, but nothing substantial. It felt as though his mind was filled with ghosts.

***

He left the office thinking about the future and how it was all laid out for him. Fight after fight, carried around the world like some kind of performing animal. Was that really all he was? Was Mr. Hammond right when he said that this flesh was the mask? In his room he opened his palms and gazed at his hands. He touched his face and traced the features of his body, and then he closed his eyes and he heard the call of the beast. He pushed it away and pressed his face into the pillow. He clutched the sheets of the bed as his mind went back to his earliest memory.

"No more! You stop there!" a man screamed. Alex whimpered. His claws scraped against the sandy ground. Pain lanced through his body as heavy chains came down, lashing against him. His legs buckled and ugly welts swelled all over his body. Blood and puss oozed out, but he had learned that he healed quickly. It only gave these people an excuse to hurt him more often. He could hear something inside him calling him, something primal and profound and all he wanted to do was listen, but these men didn't want him too. Every time he started to fall deeper into his soul he was whipped. The heavy metal bit into his skin and pain bloomed over every part of his body until he learned to control himself.

When he did well, he was rewarded with food. When he did badly, he was whipped.

He soon learned.

Mr. Hammond had trained him well.

It was the only thing he had ever known, but his eyes had been opened and he wondered if he should have been subjected to this treatment. Ben seemed to think it was wrong, but who could Alex trust? Mr. Hammond wasn't telling him anything that he truly wanted to know, but how was he going to go about finding out the truth? Who else would know? His mind was filled with questions. They flooded his thoughts and made it impossible to think about anything else. It felt as though he was floating through an abyss. The only person who knew for sure was Mr. Hammond and he seemed to be determined to keep the truth from Alex. Was it really for his own benefit, or did Mr. Hammond have his own agenda?

Alex had already begun to worry about that before he had spoken to Ben, and what Ben said had deepened his doubts. Was this place just a prison?

He clawed at his scalp, wishing that he could tear the troubled thoughts from his mind. He knew that the truth had to be in there somewhere, but why was it hiding? He ended up driving himself into such emotional turmoil that he fell asleep, where his dreams poured out of him with all their traumatic tendencies.

***

The night was obsidian black. The forest was filled with shadows. Alex was aware of everyone around him and he knew what was coming next, yet when he tried to warn them the words would not come out of his mouth. It was as though his lips had been stitched together. He looked around at the faces. They were shrouded in shadows, and no matter how fervently he stared he could not make out any distinguishing features. Perhaps that was for the best because they would die. But not him.

Why?

What made him special?

"Look up at her Alex. Isn't she beautiful?" a voice said. A figure was beside him. Her touch was gentle, her voice familiar, yet when he had heard it before it was terse with desperation and fear. Alex lifted his head and gazed to the sky. Suddenly the darkness drifted away and it was replaced by the glowing light of the moon, full and supple, like a mother's bosom. "She looks down on us, no matter what, and she connects us all. No matter where you are or what happens to us, I want you to know that you can look to the moon and be with us."

Her voice trembled with emotion. Did she know what was happening too?

Alex turned his gaze from the moon to the figure beside him. He stared at her face. The shadows swirled like a dark mist and seemed to take shape. Alex's breath caught in his throat as for the first time he thought he might actually see the face of this mysterious figure. There were hollow shapes where the eyes were, and a line formed that was a mouth, but just as these became more detailed there were roars in the background. Bright shafts of light slashed through the darkness. Panic took hold and those around him started to shift...just like him.

But before he could investigate further dark figures poured out of the darkness and fear took hold. He didn't know precisely what was happening, but he knew that something was being destroyed, something sacred and precious. There were strange sounds around him, but the one that stayed the most was a howl that seemed to reach deep into his soul.

When Alex awoke, he found that his pillow and his cheeks were wet with tears. He had no idea who he was crying for; he only knew that it was someone important. It felt as though his heart was breaking again and again, a million times over, and he was left grasping in the darkness, searching for someone forgotten and mysterious.

He needed help. If Mr. Hammond wasn't going to help him, then he would have to find someone who would. He opened the drawer to his bedside table and pulled out Ben's card. The sharp edges pressed into his palm. Alex needed answers. He couldn't live like this any longer. He couldn't do as Mr. Hammond asked and forget about all these things.

Chapter Eight

"You should have seen him Amelia. My heart breaks for him, it really does," Ben began. He was sitting with Amelia in a café, enjoying a caramel latte before they headed into the office.

"What was he like?"

"Just so...sad really. It's like he's incomplete, like his life is missing a piece. Hammond has really done a number on him. He came after me purely because he thought I might know something more about him, because of the drawing. He's searching for answers, and clearly Hammond isn't giving him anything."

"And Hammond must know more than he's letting on. Where would he even get someone like this?" Amelia asked, shaking her head.

"I take it you haven't turned anything up on Cyan yet?"

"Not yet, but I'm working on it. So what else did this guy say?"

"Not much really, just that Hammond wants him to fight. He said that Hammond won't tell him anything about his past. Whether that's because Hammond doesn't know himself or because he's deliberately withholding information I don't know, but I'm inclined to believe the former. I don't think Hammond would have someone like him and not know where he came from."

"I agree. This has to go deeper than some fight club."

"Hammond is basically keeping him prisoner. It makes me sick."

"Do you think he'll get back in touch with you?"

"I hope so," Ben said gravely, "but if not then I'm going to go back there and find a way to talk to him."

"Even though Hammond will turn you away as soon as he sees you?"

Ben lifted his gaze and met Amelia's eyes with an earnest look. His flinty eyes glowed cobalt and a strong, determined look burned within them.

"Even then. I can't just let him live this horrible life. He's in pain, even if he doesn't know it yet. There must have been some trauma in his life and I wouldn't be surprised if Hammond weren't at the middle of it. Either Alex is repressing his memories or something is repressing his memories for him."

"It's a hell of a thing you've got us messed up in," Amelia said.

"You can still back out any time you like," Ben grinned, wearing an apologetic look on his face.

"Hell no, the more I hear about this the more I'm convinced that Cyan has something to do with it. This has shady corporation written all over it, and if my hunch is right then Alex is just the tip of the iceberg. It wouldn't surprise me if there are more of them out there."

"No, but the more we talk about this the more I'm worried about how we're going to present this to William. All we have so far are rumors and speculation. There's nothing actually concrete about any of this."

Amelia reached across the table and took his hand. Hers was still warm from where it had been wrapped around her coffee mug. She flashed him a reassuring smile. "Just remember that at the core of this story is a guy who has been through a lot, and who is in pain. That's the only fact we have to be concerned about, and it's the only one that William should worry about too."

Ben was glad of her support, but he only wished it were that easy.

***

Unfortunately, when they got to the office Ben found that William wasn't in the best mood. The story had broken that Hammond was involved in an illegal fight club, and of course he had denied the whole thing. William was pacing around his office for the entire morning. His face was red and Ben wouldn't have been surprised if steam had risen from his ears. Eventually he stormed out of his office and paced around the cluster of staff.

"Well, this is it, we're in a damned war," he growled. "I knew he'd get frustrated about this story, but I never expected him to fire back like this. That story of yours ruffled feathers," William looked directly at Ben, "and now he's fighting back. He's suing us for defamation of character and he's basically saying that you're lying. He's trying to discredit you so that nobody believes the allegations against him. There are some obscure laws that he's dredged up about trespassing and other legal minutiae that is designed to keep cases in court for years on end. It's all a load of bull and I wish I could just tell him to shove it. Of course, it's not as though anyone is questioning how he can afford to keep these lawyers on a retainer when he only owns one small bar downtown, oh no, that's not suspicious at all," William threw his hands up and rolled his eyes. "And of course, being the good, honorable citizen he is he's made his bar's financial records available for our perusal so we can

62

see that there are no payments coming from any fight club."

"Wait, isn't the point that this fight club is off the books so there wouldn't be a paper trail?" Amelia asked.

"Of course it is!" William yelled. "Anyone in their right mind would know that, but the legal system is so messed up this is apparently a valid counter argument to the allegations. Apparently they're arguing that the scope of this fight club is such that it would require significant investment and adaption to the existing structure of the building, so companies would have to have been hired, and his lawyers are trying to argue that it was such a huge undertaking the only way to achieve this level of fraud would be to funnel it through the company. It's as though they've thought of everything, and of course now they're just going to try and wait out the courts and negotiate some kind of settlement. It makes me sick, it really does. God...it's times like these when it's so easy to be jaded about the world."

"But surely there has to be something else we can do? I mean, I was there, this can't just end here," Ben said, looking around in disbelief.

"It's out of our hands now," William said.

"Maybe there's something in the financial records, something they've overlooked," Amelia said.

"Good luck," William huffed on his way back to his office. Ben glanced at Amelia. This was certainly not the way they had expected this story to go. It had all seemed so simple, but a man like Hammond was used to slipping through the fingers of justice. Ben pushed his chair back and followed William into his office.

"I don't need to hear you saying what's already on my mind. Yes, I know it's unfair. Yes, I know the system is messed up. Yes, I know that there's no point us reporting on these stories when the courts fail us. I've been struggling with these kinds of thoughts all my life. I miss being your age, when you're young you think everything is going to work out alright; that the bad guys get their comeuppance and the good guys ride off into the sunset and everyone lives happily ever after. But instead it's all just one big mess." He gesticulated wildly with his hands and his tone was harsh. Ben had a lot of sympathy for him because William had been trying to nail Hammond for years and finally when he thought he had him dead to rights there were yet more tricks to try and twist his way out of his fate.

"Actually I wasn't going to say that. I was going to say that there's another way to get Hammond," Ben said.

William stopped pacing and stared at Ben. Ben took this as a gesture to continue.

"We can get him on kidnapping and imprisonment. I spoke to the person I told you about, the fighter-"

"Oh yes, your beast man," William rolled his eyes. "I've already had enough dark humor for today Ben, I don't need any more. I told you to forget about that."

"But I can't forget about him William. I don't care that you don't believe me. This is the truth. I saw him with my own eyes and I spoke with him myself. Hammond trapped him and is making him fight against his will. He's done something to this guy's memory. Alex doesn't know where he came from or who he is. I'm telling you that there's something really strange about this and Hammond deserves to pay for it. He can't treat people like this. Alex is in pain. He doesn't want to fight and yet he feels as though he has no choice because Hammond is controlling him. We should help him find out who he is, and maybe he can help us get more dirt on Hammond."

William's ears pricked up at this. "You think he'd be willing to do that?"

Ben gulped. Alex had spoken about Hammond as though he was a father, but he also knew that William wouldn't sign off on this unless he felt there was a decent chance at getting a result. "I'm sure once I've spoken to him again he will be. He's scared at the moment. The only world he knows is the one that Hammond has given him. I'm sure that once he sees there's more out there he'll understand what's at stake."

William nodded and stroked his chin. Then, he pointed towards Ben.

"If you want to go down this route then fine, but you have to listen to me when I tell you that you need to leave out this angle of the beast. I don't care what you saw or what you believe is true; it's going to ruin the rest of the story. People can only accept so much. Get the facts, get him on record. Get everyone to see what a monster he is and then we'll try to see him wriggle out of that," William said with relish.

Ben left the office and glanced towards Amelia, and that look told her everything she needed to know.

***

Ben was woken in the middle of the night by a hammering on his door. He had been up late trying to figure out his next move, for he knew that if he went back to Hammond's establishment he would only be turned away. Perhaps there was a way for him to send Alex a message, as he wasn't confident that Alex would get in touch with him. It was hard to break out of a situation like that even when you were presented with the facts. Hammond was all that Alex knew. It was going to be a challenge to make him see the possibilities of the world.

When the hammering started at the door, Ben's heart was seized by fear. His first thought was that Hammond had sent men to come and beat some sense into him. It wasn't the most difficult thing to think about; it was Ben's name on the article that had revealed Hammond's schemes after all. Ben grabbed a baseball bat as he walked out into his lounge. His feet were silent as he approached the door, and then quickly peeked through the peephole.

He breathed a sigh of relief when he saw that it was Amelia.

"What are you doing here at this time of night? I thought you were Hammond's men!" he said in a terse whisper as he ushered her in, although he did look up and down the hallway just in case anyone was lurking, but thankfully there wasn't.

Amelia carried a huge stack of files with her and dumped them on the couch. She immediately went to the kitchen and grabbed something to eat.

"I lost track of time. Haven't had dinner. You need to look in there," Amelia said, her words being lost among a mouthful of food as she gestured towards the couch. Ben placed the baseball bat against some shelves and walked towards the couch, furrowing his brow and running his hand through his hair. He wore loose pajama pants and a white t shirt.

Amelia was still in the clothes she had been wearing when he had left the office. He picked up the folder and balked when he saw a load of tables and numbers and names.

"What is this?" he asked. Amelia swallowed and then poured herself a glass of milk, gulping it down eagerly. A film of white liquid was left around her upper lip, which she wiped away instantly.

"That, my friend, is the key to all of this." She strode over to the couch and took the folder from Ben. She threw herself down and patted the chair beside him, gesturing for him to join her, which he did so, although he was still puzzled by the dramatic entrance. She leafed through and picked out a few sheets of paper. On these she had highlighted certain names.

"Okay," she continued, "so when William said that Hammond had made his financial records available for us to look at, I thought he might have overlooked something. Arrogance always leads to a downfall and it's not like most people are going to go through them with a fine tooth comb. While it might not have pointed to a fight club, there still might have been something in there that would help us. Anyway, I found this." She grinned triumphantly as she handed Ben a few pieces of paper. He scanned them all. The name she highlighted was a company name, 'Blue Banner Inc' and it appeared a number of times, all with a substantial amount of money being invested into Hammond's company.

"What is this?" he asked.

"That's what I thought. I looked through the major transactions that appeared on his statements. Most of them were the things you'd expect, like food and alcohol and all that kind of thing, but this one was for miscellaneous goods and that didn't seem quite right to me. So I looked up this company and it seems to be a design company, focusing on software and websites, and it didn't seem as though Hammond would be involved in something like this. So then I did some more digging and it turns out, well, I'll show you," her eyes gleamed as she pulled out her phone and handed it to him. He looked at the webpage. At first, he didn't see anything wrong with it, but then he scanned the small print and when he saw what Amelia wanted him to see, his blood ran cold and his stomach twisted into a knot.

"Blue Banner is a subsidiary of Cyan Enterprises," Ben said. Amelia nodded.

"Cyan is involved with this. I knew it from the beginning. He's tied up with them somehow."

"Okay, but let's hold on here. Just because he's linked with Cyan it doesn't mean that this is anything to do with Alex. We have to act like William here and look at the facts."

"Here's a fact. Look at when the payments started. If you can find out when Alex started appearing at the bar, you might find a link there."

The payments had started about a year ago. Ben nodded as his mind whirred. This was exciting and scary all at the same time. Trying to unravel a conspiracy like this was every journalist's dream, but the ramifications were scary. It was one thing to go after a man like Hammond, but to go after Cyan...it opened a whole new world of problems. Ben took a deep breath and held open his palms.

"Okay, before we go any further, are we sure we want to do this?"

Amelia glared at him. There were dark shadows under her eyes. Her green eyes glared at him with the intensity of a burning sun.

"I can't believe you're actually asking me that. This needs to be chased up. If there is a link between the two then we need to find out what it is. If Cyan is doing some weird experiments with people, then they need to be exposed. This is a dystopian nightmare Ben. A corporation has gotten so big it thinks it can do anything, even play God. We need to find out what's going on, and it's going to be the only way we can help Alex."

Ben nodded. "Okay, what's our next move?"

"I'll work my sources, you work yours. Try and get close to Alex. He might know more than he realizes."

Ben nodded again. His thoughts turned to that tortured soul and he hoped that this wouldn't lead him into more danger. He also wondered how he was going to get in touch with Alex if he couldn't get close to Hammond's place, but as it happened, he didn't have to do a thing.

Chapter Nine

Alex didn't want to make a habit of sneaking out without Mr. Hammond knowing, but he needed to see Ben for his own sanity. His mind was tortured and the thought of fighting over and over again was too much to bear. The light was fading as the evening turned into night. They met by the lake again. A few people were still out by the boats. Alex wondered what it would be like to sail out there. He'd never been sailing before.

"I'm glad you called," Ben said. He wore a hooded jacket and had his hands dug deep into his pockets. He glanced around furtively and pulled Alex to one side. "We should go somewhere nobody can hear us." Alex nodded and followed him to the boat house. The swarthy man eyed them up and told them the price. Ben shoved a few crumpled notes into his hand and then gestured to the boat. Although Alex looked hesitant, he tried not to reveal that side of him to Ben.

They climbed in the boat, which was a small, narrow boat containing two oars. It was shaky as they got in, and Alex almost lost his balance. Ben smirked and took hold of the oars, guiding them away from the edge of the lake towards the middle of the expanse of water. There were a few other people rowing out, idly enjoying the experience of being out upon the water, and the lake was big enough that they could row to a place that was far away from anyone else. Ben rowed them to the middle of the lake and then pulled the oars in, letting them drift on top of the still water. All around the park stretched out, its natural beauty comforting and reassuring, although Alex wasn't sure why he felt this way.

"Why did you call me?" Ben asked.

Alex cleared his throat. It had been one thing to think about calling Ben, but quite another to go through with it.

"I was thinking about what you said. When I went back home Mr. Hammond called me in for a meeting and told me that he had plans for me. He said that he was going to make me a star and that a lot of people wanted to see me fight. When I told him that I wasn't sure I wanted to fight he looked at me as if I was mad. He told me that nothing else mattered apart from the fights and that I was…that I was nothing when I wasn't fighting. When I asked him who I was and how he found me he said that none of that mattered, and this was just a mask. He said that when I was a beast that was the true me. You were right in that. He never gave me a choice and I still don't know where I'm from or what I'm doing here. All I want is some answers and if he can't give me any then I need to find someone who can." He looked at Ben directly, with an earnest look in his eyes, and whole lot of hope as well.

Ben nodded and pursed his lips. He gazed out at the lake.

"I used to come here when I was a kid. My folks brought me out here quite a lot. It was peaceful, and a way to escape life. It felt like stepping into another world. I could come out here and float on this lake and leave all my troubles behind. I used to close my eyes and pretend that I was sailing near an island somewhere, far out in the ocean where nobody could come and get me. This is the most important place in my life, and it's where, one day, Mom and Dad brought me here and told me a secret. They told me I was adopted. I'd never even given it a second thought at that point. They were Mom and Dad, and I was their kid. But they told me that it was time for me to know and I had to make a decision; did I want to meet my biological Mom? Well, it was a lot to put on a kid," he said. Alex waited for him to continue.

"Did you meet her?"

"I did. And I was...I think it meant more to her than it did to me. She was so filled with hope. I think that she thought it was going to be the beginning of this wonderful reunion where she could make up for the mistakes of the past. She apologized profusely and told me why she put me up for adoption, but all the time she was talking I was sitting there thinking that she was just a stranger, just some woman I had no connection with. I had a Mom and Dad, and I didn't need another one." He clenched his jaw and reached out of the boat, dipping his fingers into the water.

"That's a sad story, but I don't know what it has to do with me," Alex said, puzzled.

"What I'm trying to say is that sometimes finding the truth hurts. Sometimes it's better to live in ignorance. I don't know where this is going to lead or what answers you're going to find. It's just that...you've been through a lot already and I want you to understand that you might have to go through a whole lot more pain before you come to the end of this. Is that something you want to do?" Ben asked. There was a harsh tone to his words, but underneath them all was something honest and worried as well. There was no real reason for Ben to care this much about his fate, and yet he did. It was endearing to Alex, and he found himself caring about Ben as well. What he had just revealed must have been difficult for him.

"You have those memories and while they're painful at least you have them. I have nothing like that. When I think of my parents I…I don't even know if I have any. The only reason I know my name is Alex is because Mr. Hammond told me that's what my name is. There's darkness where my life should be. I need to find out. I don't care if my story is painful or sad, because that's better than looking into myself and finding nothing."

"Last time we spoke you mentioned you had dreams?" Ben asked in a gentle tone.

"They're just dreams. They don't mean anything."

"What if they're your memories trying to get out?" Ben asked. Alex swallowed. Part of him had been afraid of that. When Alex didn't respond, Ben spoke again. "Look, if we're going to go through this, we're going to need to trust each other. I know you don't have much experience of the world, but you could be in a very dangerous situation."

"What do you mean?" Alex asked, frowning. The dying embers of light were in paintbrush streaks across the sky as the sun retreated below the horizon and made way for the moon to take the celestial throne. The ripples of the water were soft and gentle. Murmured voices drifted over the lake from the other people in the boats, although what they said was unintelligible. Ben had a grave expression on his face.

"This might be difficult for you to hear. I don't know all the details, but I think there's a big…*thing* going on. Mr. Hammond isn't as nice as you think. He's involved in a lot of shady things, like illegal gambling, money laundering, theft, bribery, too many to list really. And all the time he's been able to get away with it because nobody has been able to pin anything on him. That's why I was at the fighting pits that night, to try and see for myself what he was up to. And now my friend has learned that he's working with a company called Cyan. They have been making payments to him. We know when these payments started, and we're wondering if they might have something to do with you. Do you know when you first became involved with Hammond?"

Alex blinked. His stomach turned. "No I...I don't."

"Think carefully Alex. This is important," Ben said.

No, it couldn't be. This was wrong.

"Are you sure about him?" Alex asked.

"As sure as I can be about anything. He's not a nice man."

But Mr. Hammond had taken him in. He had taught Alex so much. He had given him a home, given him purpose.

"What if...what if Mr. Hammond saved me from this Cyan company?" Alex said, eager to cling onto anything that was steady when so much of his life had crumbled away.

"Then why would he be getting payments from them? We think he's still working with them now, that's why he can afford to have so many expensive lawyers helping him. But with your help we can bring him down. We can make him pay for all he's done and we can find out exactly what happened with you."

Pain throbbed in Alex's mind. Suddenly the boat seemed very, very small. His skin prickled and his chest tightened. Mr. Hammond's words echoed through his mind; the past doesn't matter, only the future matters, only he could help Alex. Maybe this was all happening as he had foreseen. He had warned Alex about Ben, had warned him not to speak to Ben and now Alex saw it too.

"You only want me to get to him, don't you? That's why you're here. You don't care about helping me or finding out my past. You only want me to remember so I can say something bad about Mr. Hammond. That's the only reason you're here," Alex said, his voice thundering as loud as his heartbeat. Pressure rang against his mind and he rose abruptly. He could feel the blood rushing inside and all he wanted was to be free, to escape.

"No, Alex, it's not like that at all. I want to help you be free of his influence because he really is not a nice man and I'm worried about you if you stay with him. Please, you have to believe me."

"No, he warned me about you. He told me that I shouldn't trust you. He was right all along. He's the only one who has wanted to help me. I need to get back. I've been away for too long. I need to accept my fate."

"No you don't," Ben said. "You just need to fight whatever he's been saying to you. I know it's hard but you need to accept the truth."

Truth. That was a funny word. When Alex looked into Ben's eyes, he saw something earnest but it was also frightening. Alex had already lost so much he wasn't sure he could turn away from the life he knew. It was the only thing he had. Could he really fling himself into darkness? His world was already unsteady, and by accepting Ben's help he would only be making things even harder on himself. No, this had been a mistake. This had all been a mistake. He should have just listened to Mr. Hammond. Yes, Mr. Hammond would take care of him.

Alex rose without thinking. All he wanted was to leave.

"Take me back!" he yelled, pointing back towards the boat house. Ben tried to protest, but Alex gesticulated wildly again, so wildly that he threw himself off balance. The boat swayed and toppled, as uncertain as his own mind. Alex felt himself being pulled. Before he could steady himself, he found himself falling out of the boat, plunging into the cold water. As soon as he broke through the cold surface his body was shocked into remembrance.

***

Alex was running through the forest, sprinting. His lungs burned with the effort. He stumbled and fell, getting a mouthful of dirt. His skin was torn and throbbed with pain, but that was nothing compared to the fear that surged through his heart. Behind him were people rampaging through the woods, firing at the shadows around him. He looked around wildly. Dark figures appeared like phantoms, clad in black outfits, wielding strange weapons. Alex had been told to run even though he was so scared, even though he wanted to fight. He knew that something horrible was happening, something that wasn't supposed to happen.

There were snarls and howls in the distance, but Alex cared for none of that. He just knew he had to get away. Branches whipped his arms and face as he ran through the forest. His heartbeat was as loud as a drum, and he could hear other people chasing him.

They cursed as they hacked and slashed their way through the forest.

Then Alex came to a lake. He threw himself into the water. It was cold and icy. The chill crept into his bones, it froze his tongue, but he felt free.

Then hands clamped down upon him, dragged him out. He kicked and screamed and he could feel something happening inside him. He was changing. The bloodlust took hold.

"Get him tranq'ed!" a man called. Pain bloomed in his back. Alex looked down and saw a dart sticking out. Everything began to grow hazy, as he was dragged back to a clearing. Trucks waited, and all around him were wolves. He looked up at the moon and a tear rolled down his cheek, and then everything went dark.

Chapter Ten

"Alex!" Ben yelled. He pushed himself to the side of the boat and reached down, grabbing Alex's arm as he thrashed in the water. With his other hand, Ben gripped onto the side of the boat, trying to keep his balance so that he didn't fall in as well. The boat jerked as Alex flailed. Ben tried to pull him up, but lacked the strength. He looked around and was struck by an idea.

"Grab this!" he cried as he pushed the oar towards Alex. Alex broke through the surface, gasping, and pulled himself back towards the boat. Water trickled down his face and body. His clothes were utterly soaked. Ben helped him back into the boat. Alex's chest was heaving as he caught his breath.

"You need to be more careful in boats," Ben said. He was angry that Alex had jeopardized himself like this, and angry that Alex seemed resistant to helping him.

"I had a vision. A memory," he panted.

That caught Ben's attention. Ben grabbed the oar and started to row back to shore, but he looked directly at Alex and asked him what he remembered.

"I was in a place like this," Alex looked around. He wiped the water off his face and seemed to be in a daze. "I was running from something...from people."

"What people?"

"I don't know. I couldn't see them. They were dressed in all black. But I knew I had to get away. I ran to some water. I dived in and I thought I had escaped. It was so cold. But then I was pulled out. I was taken back and they did something to me, something to make me sleep. That's all I remember." His voice trailed away and it cracked with emotion. He looked utterly desolate and Ben's heart went out to him. What Alex said before, about not knowing his past, really struck a chord with Ben. There had been many times when Ben had wished that he had forgotten certain things, but that had never been a possibility.

Ben leaned forward and took Alex's hand. It trembled, and his palm was slick with water.

"I'm here for you Alex. I'll help you find out what happened. I promise."

Alex nodded. Ben let the gesture linger, feeling the warmth seeping through the water. He gazed into Alex's eyes and a profound feeling swept through him. A smile played upon Ben's lips and his heart swelled at the thought of helping him. Eventually he released Ben's hand and rowed the boat back to the shore. He helped Alex out. The poor guy was still shivering. Ben took off his jacket and wrapped it around Alex's shoulders, hoping that would go some way to shielding him from the chill.

"I don't live far from here. Come back with me and I'll help you get warmed up, and we can talk more about this," Ben suggested. He was relieved when Alex agreed.

***

Ben opened the door to his apartment and showed Alex in. He grabbed a towel and a change of clothes, telling Alex to just chuck the wet clothes into the laundry basket. Ben waited for him to get dry and changed. As he did so, he made some cocoa and ruminated on what he had learned. It definitely seemed that this was bigger than Hammond. But surely if there had been a raid in some forest somewhere, someone would have noticed it? Ben had a lot to tell Amelia the next time they saw each other, although he refrained from telling her now because he wanted to focus on Alex. It was a delicate business. Ben's hunger to bring down Hammond and reveal the truth about his connection with Cyan had to come second to Alex's wellbeing. This wasn't just some game, it was his life. If Ben made the wrong move it might push Alex away, as it had done in the boat. He had to approach this not just as a reporter, but as a person. In this instance it wasn't a difficult adjustment as he found himself intrigued by Alex, drawn to him in a way that he wasn't usually drawn to anyone.

Of course, that would bring complications by itself and he tried to tell himself to push aside those feelings before they could become a factor, but his heart never usually listened to his head.

Alex emerged looking a lot better. His hair was still flecked with water and clung to his scalp, but otherwise he was dry and he had stopped shivering. Still, Ben wanted to make sure that he wasn't going to suffer anything like pneumonia, so he made sure that Alex had a blanket and a mug of hot cocoa. Alex smiled in gratitude and sipped the hot drink, the steam rising around his face.

"I'm sorry about before. I didn't mean to make you feel uncomfortable," Ben said, settling on the couch beside Alex.

Alex shook his head. "You shouldn't have to apologize. I reacted badly. It's just that this is difficult for me. I don't know myself, and I so I don't know who I can trust. I don't know what's right and what's wrong."

"I think you do. Even if you can't remember who you are you must still have some kind of morality. You know that fighting is wrong after all," Ben said.

Alex nodded. "Perhaps you're right. I just wish I knew what all this meant."

"It might come back, in time, or there may be other triggers. Jumping in the water brought back memories. There might be other things that will bring back other memories. We just have to experiment and see what they are, but it might be a long process and we should be careful about it. I don't want to do anything that overwhelms you."

"No me neither," Alex sipped his cocoa and had a thoughtful look on his face. Ben could see the pain in his expression and his heart melted once again.

"You know, I don't tell too many people that story about how I found out I was adopted," Ben said. Alex looked up, meeting his gaze.

"Then why did you tell me?"

"Because I wanted you to know that you're not alone in having mixed feelings about your past. I wanted you to know that you can trust me."

"You told me that I might not want to know the truth of my past. Is that because you didn't want to know?"

Ben nodded and looked solemn. His head dipped and he wrung his fingers. "Up until that point I had been living a normal life with normal parents who loved me. I never had any doubt about my place in the world. And then I was told that I was adopted. For a long time I hated them for that, my adoptive parents I mean. I thought they should have kept it to themselves. I couldn't understand why they wanted to ruin what we had. It tainted everything. When I looked at them before they were Mom and Dad, but after that they were just these two people who had taken on a kid that nobody wanted. And I had to cope with knowing that my birth parents didn't want me. I was worthless to them, unwanted, how is that supposed to make me feel?"

"When you met her, did your mother tell you why she put you up for adoption?"

Ben nodded. "The usual reasons really. She was young, didn't know how to handle it. The guy she was dating left her as soon as he found out she was pregnant with me. She just didn't have room in her life for me. I spoke to my parents about it and they told me that they didn't adopt me because they took pity on me. They said that I was a gift. Mom...she couldn't have kids and they had always wanted one, but adoption had never worked out. Then I came along. They called me a little miracle, but I could never forget that deep down I wasn't wanted. It took me a long time to come to terms with that. To be honest I'm not sure that I have. But it's why I became a reporter, because I might as well be the one hunting for the truth if it's so important for people to hear it."

"It must have been hard for you, to have your whole world change like that. I'm afraid of it happening to me. I'm afraid of what we're going to find at the end of this.

"I know," Ben sighed. "I wish it were easier. I wish Hammond would tell you what he knows."

"He just wants me to fight. He says that he's got fights lined up all over the world and people are going to want to pay to see me. He seems to think that I can win all of them."

"You probably can, given what you can do."

"Do you think there are others like me?" Alex asked. His eyes glistened with an innocent sorrow that stabbed right into Ben's heart.

"I don't know," Ben answered honestly. "And if there are, we need to get to the truth of this for their sake as well. You ended up with Mr. Hammond, but who knows where others would end up. But even if you are the only person like this it doesn't mean that you're alone." Ben reached out and placed his hand upon Alex's. His skin was warm now, vibrant with life and energy. The feeling of being in contact with him was comforting and invigorating all at once.

"Can I see the drawing again?" Alex asked, his voice sounded like a choking sob.

Ben pulled out the drawing and handed it to Alex. He took it and studied it carefully.

"I'd never really seen myself before I saw this drawing. I look so…so horrible," his lips turned into a snarl and his grip tightened on the page, so much so that the paper started to tremble.

"No, you don't," Ben said. "You look powerful. You look strong. I couldn't take my eyes off you when I saw you."

"You weren't scared?" Alex asked, taking his eyes off the drawing. Ben sidled closer towards him and put the drawing aside. He slipped his hand into Alex's, feeling the comfortable heat taking hold of him. Something about this just seemed right.

"I was scared of what you might do, but I wasn't scared of the way you looked. If anything I was intrigued. I wanted to know who you were and how this had happened to you. I wanted to know if you were in pain. I wanted...I wanted to be close to you."

"You're close to me now," Alex said. There was hesitancy in his voice, but there was something else in his eyes, something that called to Ben. His soft lips were parted and looked inviting. Ben tilted his head and leaned in, then pressed his mouth against Alex. There was a rush of warm, sweet breath, and then an explosion of pleasure. Alex kissed back. A hand rested on Ben's hips. Ben's hand rose up and curled around the nape of Alex's neck, playing with the damp hair.

"Are you trying to find another trigger for a memory?" Alex whispered.

"Maybe," Ben grinned. "We can stop if you like," he placed a hand upon Alex's chest. Alex paused for a moment, but then shook his head. He smiled and kissed Ben again. The two men wrapped their arms around each other as they drowned in their embrace. Heat rose and the air sizzled. Ardent lips pressed against each other and eager tongues darted out, dancing in the heat of the night. Ben's hands roamed around Alex's body, feeling his way across the vibrant flesh. He kissed along Alex's jawline and against his neck. His breath was hot and made Alex tremble as it rushed against his skin. Ben tugged at the shirt, and Alex made similar movements, responding in kind.

Arousal simmered and Ben could feel it twitching. He reached down and brushed his hand across Alex's lap. Alex trembled and laughed nervously.

"It's okay," Ben whispered. "If you're unsure..."

Alex grabbed Ben's hand and thrust it down hard into his lap, groaning slightly.

"It feels so good," Alex said. Alex moved his hand over Ben's lap and they started to massage each other. There was an uncertainty to Alex's touch that Ben found endearing and attractive. He needn't have been nervous as he seemed naturally attuned to pleasuring Ben. Their deep moans rippled through the air and the cocoa grew cold as they groped each other, pulling at each other's shirts. Soon all manner of speech was lost as they descended into this wonderful abyss. Pleasure danced around Ben's mind as he succumbed to the call of his body. His kisses became harder, his touch became firmer, and his hands began to explore more. He leaned back and pulled off his shirt, before he did the same to Alex. They sat on the couch, running their hands across the expanse of each other's bodies. They traced every line of defined muscle, laughed as they found each other's sweet spots, and delighted in every tremble they caused.

They were like painters working with a fresh canvas, creating a landscape of lust. As Ben ran his hands down the middle of Alex's torso, he was amazed to wonder how there was a beast locked inside him. It may have been weird and wild, but Ben wasn't turned off by it at all. He kissed Alex passionately as his hand drove down even deeper and started to unclasp Alex's jeans. Alex groaned and leaned back, watching as Ben got to work, and then Alex fumbled with Ben's jeans. It became a race to see which man could free the other first, but they ended up opening themselves at the same time. Ben stood up and pushed down his jeans, as well as his underwear, while Alex remained on the couch and wriggled out of his.

Alex's mouth was agape as Ben stripped for him, and there was a look of awe on his face as Ben unleashed his manhood. Ben was pleased to see that Alex was also blessed with a long and thick erection. Heat and lust flowed through Ben's body. He stepped forward and reached out to run his hand along Alex's scalp. Alex groaned as he was pulled forward. His willing lips hung open and when they touched the smooth, sensitive tip Ben groaned loudly. His neck arched back. Alex closed his eyes and slid down deeper, taking more of Ben in his mouth. The wetness and the heat were exhilarating and Ben felt the release of pleasure slipping through his entire body. Alex's tongue danced around, creating a whirl of delight in Ben's mind. Ben's body trembled and he knew he couldn't take much more. It had been so long, and he had never had anyone as good as Alex.

Ben kept a strong hand on Alex's head. The smooth rhythm made the tension rise within his body. It coiled like a serpent and hissed with passionate venom. Flames licked at his soul and sweat trickled down the middle of his chest. He looked down at moaned at the sight of Alex making love to him. The kisses were soft, the flicks of the tongue were deft and delicate, while the sucks were deep and longing. Ben could feel the twitching and the throbbing inside him. His groans grew deeper and his grip tightened even more as he whispered to Alex. His eyes clamped shut as the pleasure threatened to explode, and then suddenly it came out in a thick burst. His body trembled as he gave Alex everything, and Alex took everything with eager gulps.

Ben sank back to the couch, sitting beside Alex, unable to be apart from him. He leaned in for a deep, passionate kiss. The sensations that swirled around his mind were chaotic and incoherent, but also wonderful and delirious. He ran his hand all over Alex's body and then started to play with Alex. He took Alex's erection in his hand, curling his fingers around the thick shaft and began stroking. He ran his thumb over the smooth mushroom tip, making Alex shudder. He traced the rippling veins that were swollen with blood and smiled with delight as the pleasure they shared was a song with no end.

Ben kissed Alex deeply and then took Alex's hand in his, bringing it to his lips. Ben sucked on Alex's fingers, coating them in his saliva, before thrusting his hand down into the deepest, most intimate part of his body. A deep sensation fluttered in the core of Ben's body and his mind grew hazy. He took his own hand and licked his palm before stroking Alex again. Within moments Alex's erection was coated in saliva and glistened like a towering rock that had been flecked by the sea.

Ben groaned as he swung his leg over Alex and lowered himself down, gently at first. He closed his eyes as he felt the pain and pleasure mix together. The tip touched him, and then as Ben lowered himself, they became one. Both men groaned. Their breaths swirled and joined. Ben curled his arms around Alex's head and kissed him deeply as he started to rock back and forth. The feeling of having Alex inside him was something that made him burn with wildfire. The scent and the heat of Alex's body were inviting. It was a place that Ben never wanted to leave. He opened his eyes and saw delight dance across Alex's face. Ben smiled and buried his head in Alex's neck, losing himself to the fervent emotions that crackled like lightning through his body. It was a passion that was deep and profound. It called to a primal part of him, a part that had been denied for too long.

He tasted Alex upon his lips and pressed his body as close as he could. The two men melted into each other. Alex's hands squeezed Ben's thighs. Ben could feel the tension rippling through Alex. He felt the shuddering anticipation and knew that heaven was going to be upon him within moments. His breath deepened and he kissed Alex even more deeply as he increased his rhythm, and then the kiss was broken as Alex moaned loudly. Warmth exploded into Ben and he felt it all seeping into him. He collapsed onto Alex, a pool of lust and passion, draped over Alex's body. Alex gasped for breath. His arms lay limp beside him, his body had been drained of strength.

Ben smiled and placed a finger under Alex's chin, tilting his head up. He placed a gentle kiss on Alex's lips and smiled, before closing his eyes and letting the last drops of pleasure fall away.

Chapter Eleven

Alex's mind was awhirl. He and Ben were splayed over the couch, a blanket draped over their bodies. Their skin still burned with the fading echo of pleasure. Alex's mind was still fervent at having experienced something so wonderful and sensual. It had been nerve-wracking at first, as he had been afraid he would do something wrong, but then it had all happened naturally. All he had to do was follow his instincts.

Now he lay wrapped in Ben's arms. He could feel the tremors of Ben's heartbeat, which were still powerful. The warmth of Ben's body was comforting and much more reassuring than the emptiness of his own bed.

"That was amazing," Ben said. Alex was glad that he had been able to make Been feel good.

"It's nice to know I'm good at something other than fighting," Alex said with a smirk. Ben chuckled and stroked Alex's cheek.

"I'm sure we'll discover plenty of things that you're good at. I don't suppose that triggered any memory?"

Alex looked down. "No, at least I don't think so. Maybe I don't have any more memories to trigger."

"Well, maybe that just means you haven't had a boyfriend before. It doesn't mean that you don't have anything left inside you. I'm sure there will be other things. Maybe tomorrow we'll go outside and walk around the city and see if anything comes to mind," Ben suggested. Alex nodded and swallowed a lump in his throat.

"I don't suppose there's anything else that might shed some light on things?" Ben asked.

"There's only one thing," Alex said. His voice trembled with uncertainty as he wasn't sure whether he should talk about it at all. It was still difficult to go against Mr. Hammond's orders even though it was clear that something was wrong with the way Mr. Hammond had treated him.

"What is it?"

"It's just that...whenever I turn into that...beast, there's something calling to me, something deep inside. I'm always tempted to answer that call, but Mr. Hammond has trained me not to. He says that I should never follow that voice and that I should just go as far as you've seen."

"You mean there's more to this transformation?" Ben asked, furrowing his brow.

Alex nodded.

"Well that's it!" Ben jerked up. His movement was so swift that he almost sent Alex crashing off the couch. "There has to be something that Hammond is afraid of you finding out. Maybe if you change fully you might be able to access some memories that have been buried. Don't you see Alex? Maybe the answer has been inside you all along, but it's just been hidden in this other side of you."

"Maybe," Alex leaned forward. His shoulders slumped and he ran his hand through his hair. The excitement went out of Ben's voice.

"I thought you would be more excited," Ben said.

"I just…I'm afraid of changing. When I turn, I don't have control. They have to drug me to keep from going on a rampage when I fight."

"What's it like? I mean, do you remember anything from when you turn?"

"I do. I know what I need to do, but it's more like I run on instinct."

"You must have some control though, otherwise surely you'd listen to this other voice inside you?"

Alex wasn't sure what to say to that. He'd never thought of it like that before.

"Did you ever think that the reason they drug you isn't to protect others from you, but to stop you from fighting back?" Ben asked. "When you're in that form you're going to be stronger than any of them. You could have ripped through those chains and escaped if you wanted to. What if it's just another way to control you? I'm willing to bet that you have more control than you think. Come on," Ben rose from the sofa and pulled on his clothes. Alex looked up at him in shock.

"What are you doing?"

"We're going to go outside and you're going to transform fully, to see if we can get this memory back.

Alex shook his head. Fear clutched at his heart.

"No, I can't do that. I can't risk it. Not out here. What if something happens? What if I hurt someone? What if I hurt you?"

"You're not going to hurt me Alex. You said yourself that you listen to your instincts, and so far, your instincts haven't told you to be afraid of me, have they?"

Alex shook his head.

"So it's going to be fine."

"But we don't know what this final transformation is going to be like. What if I turn into an even greater beast and I do lose control? I can't risk it Ben. I'm not willing to hurt you."

Ben smiled at him and reached out to cup his head. "That's really sweet Alex, and it means a lot to me, but if I'm right this might be the only way to remember what really happened to you. I trust you."

Alex's heart skipped a beat when he heard these words. It helped to erode the fear that swam in the pit of his stomach. He had been conditioned to hate the beast inside him, but now Ben actually wanted it freed. Maybe it was time that Alex trusted someone other than Mr. Hammond. Maybe it was time he trusted himself.

He nodded, and Ben smiled.

"It's going to be okay, I promise," Ben said, gripping Alex's hand. Alex wished it was a promise Ben was able to keep.

***

They walked outside and went back to the park. By this time of night it was deserted, only populated by shadows and nocturnal animals. They walked into a secret place that was surrounded by trees and hidden from the rest of the world. There was a small gap through the canopy where the stars were visible, and where the moon held its silent vigil. At the sight of it, Alex's soul was calmed. The moon offered safety.

"Are you sure you want to do this here? If something goes wrong there's not going to be anyone around to save you," Alex said.

"I'm sure. Nothing is going to go wrong. Hammond hasn't told you the truth about yourself Alex. He's been afraid of you and he's tried to control you. We can't trust anything he says. I believe in you, and you have to believe in yourself. When you change you just need to listen to your heart. There's no danger out here. I'm not going to hurt you and you don't have to fight anyone. That's the only thing that matters. This way you change, it's not like it's some other force. It's still you, it's just another side of you. That's why I'm not scared Alex. I know you won't hurt me."

Alex nodded. Ben seemed so sure of himself. Alex only wished he had the same level of confidence. But if this was the key to his past then he had to take it. The whisper had been harder to resist recently and it was only to loyalty to Mr. Hammond that Alex had found the strength to quell the urge to give in. But Mr. Hammond had also made it clear he didn't care about Alex, only what Alex could do for him. Ben was the one who tried to get to the heart of the matter, and he trusted Alex when nobody else would.

Alex nodded and walked to the middle of the clearing, taking a deep breath as he did so. He closed his eyes while Ben remained at the edge of the trees. Alex listened to his heartbeat and felt the blood rushing through him. So far, he had only shifted when he was in danger, when pain had fueled his every movement. This was different. He looked inside himself, searched for the whisper among the silence. Like the moon on a dark night it was a beacon of light, a guide that showed him the direction to salvation.

Alex let it wind through his mind. As he breathed, he gradually felt himself changing. Pain blurred into sweet anguish as he felt his body changing. The world around him started to change too.

Suddenly he could feel more of the world. He could taste the sweetness of the night air and he was intoxicated by the fragrance of the flowers. In the distance he could hear an animal scurrying away. Its heartbeat fluttered on the air. And there was something else, yes, someone else.

Ben.

Alex's heart flared with anger at first. He was so used to the presence of anyone else being a sign of danger. He snarled and snapped his jaws together. His claws were pointed and sharp, and his limbs trembled, ready for a fight. But then something reminded him that he didn't have to fight this time. The fighting was over. The anger was quelled and the furor inside him died down, and all that was left was a whisper.

A whisper he had been taught to ignore.

At first, he winced when he heard it, for the memories of being lashed and whipped with chains were still strong in his mind. He whimpered and backed away. His mind was filled with Mr. Hammond's voice telling him to retreat, to forget the whisper and maintain this form. It was so hard though when the whisper was so tempting.

This time there were no chains. After Alex flinched, he remembered that Ben was here. He opened his eyes and breathed in the air. The scent was comforting, and it reassured him that he wasn't lashing out at everything. Mr. Hammond had been wrong. He was more than a fighter. The whisper called to him, and this time he followed it. He ran deeper into his soul and embraced whatever was waiting for him there.

His body changed again. His skin burned as fur spread out and grew through his pores. He collapsed down so that he was standing on all fours, and his mouth turned fully into a snout. He looked up at the moon, and he howled. It was something that came naturally to him, as though it was bred into his blood, passed down, a legacy of the soul. He howled, and it was lamentable. He howled for all he had lost and for all that he would never know, but as he did so something was triggered in the back of his mind. The moon seemed to throb as he gazed at it, and then it too shifted. The mottled, round shape shifted. The cratered shadows became eyes that swam with kindness and the night behind it flowed around like dark hair, until it was fully the form of a woman, a face that he recognized somewhere inside him.

And then a memory took hold.

***

"Look at the moon Alex. She is your guiding light. Whenever you have doubt, whenever you are scared, look to the moon. She will guide you wherever you are. We are children of the moon, and she will never forsake us."

Alex looked up. Once again, he was in a memory. He wanted to yell and shout, to warn her about what was happening, but he could not. He was almost afraid to look up and see another shadowed face, but this time he could actually see her, and he was struck by how beautiful she was, as beautiful as the moon itself. Her skin was pale, her eyes wide and dark, her voice was lilting and her hair flowed down in a dark veil. There was something else that was familiar about her as well, but that remained elusive.

"This world is not an easy one for us to live in Alex. I wish that things had been better. I wish that we had lived in a different time, a time when we could be free to roam the horizon as we once did without being troubled by humans. There are dangers lurking nearby and I hope that you can forgive your father and I for bringing you into this world. It was not a curse. It is not a punishment. We brought you into this world because we love you, and we love each other. I'm only sorry that we can't give you the life you deserve, the life we wanted to give you."

Her voice choked on her emotions. She touched his cheek and then looked up at the moon again. His mother! Alex wanted to cry out and speak with her. He wanted to reach out and touch her as well.

"There's so much I want to tell you. So much that I can't because I know that you won't understand. Just promise me that if you ever find a chance to be happy you must take it with everything you have, because happiness is all too fleeting these days. I wish there was more I could tell you, but just remember to be true to yourself. Listen to your heart, and look to the moon. The moon will always be with you Alex, even if I can't."

The ground trembled underneath him and loud shouts burst forth from the forest. The attack was happening again. She turned to him and told him to run. Everything in Alex's mind told him to stay, but he wasn't really there. This was just a memory. She was gone...

***

Alex felt sick inside as he retreated from the memory. He trembled all over. He pawed at the ground and looked up at the moon again, letting out one last howl, a mournful howl filled with sorrow that would have broken the heart of anyone who had heard it. Slowly, the fur receded from his body and his paws turned back into hands and feet. His snout retreated back to a mouth. He fell back into a sitting position and tears rolled down his cheeks. Ben rushed to him.

"I saw her Ben. I saw my Mom," he said, his voice trembling with emotion.

Chapter Twelve

Ben wasn't sure how he would ever describe what he had just seen. Despite his insistence that he trusted Alex, there was still an element of fear that ran through him when Alex shifted. He turned into the same beast Ben had seen before in the arena. He was huge, a hulking mass of muscle and power. But then he changed again. The tufts of fur lengthened and grew out until they covered his whole body. His clawed hands turned into paws, and his eyes became beady. He was a wolf, bigger than any wolf Ben had ever seen before, but a wolf, nonetheless. And then he had howled at the moon. The howls tore at Ben's soul and he was filled with such pity that he almost cried himself.

When Alex returned to the form of a man, Ben rushed towards him and wrapped his arms around him. He cradled Alex and wiped the tears from his eyes.

"What do you mean you saw her? Did you have another memory?"

Alex nodded. "She told me that I was a child of the moon, that we were all children of the moon. She said...she said that she was sorry she couldn't give me the life she wanted to give me. And then we were attacked. But before, in the other memory, I saw a lot of wolves being carried away too."

"You are a wolf Alex. The biggest wolf I've ever seen."

"I didn't...I didn't hurt you, did I?"

"No," Ben said grinning, "and you didn't scare me either. You looked wonderful, majestic even." He kissed Alex in an effort to reassure him. "Thank you for sharing that with me."

"But what does it mean? Why am I like this?"

"You must be a werewolf. It's the only explanation. I always thought they were just a myth but I can't deny what I've seen with my own eyes."

"The woman…Mom," Alex's voice cracked when he said this. "She told me there was a time when we roamed across the land without being disturbed. She said that I was born at the wrong time."

"Maybe you were," Ben said. His brow furrowed as he started thinking about what this meant, and why Cyan might have gotten involved. There were still missing pieces to the puzzle, but it was slowly falling into place.

"But you know what this means, don't you?" he asked. Alex looked at him blankly. "Whatever this is, it's a part of you and it has been from birth. And that means there are other people out there like you. We just have to find them. Maybe your Mom is still out there somewhere as well. It means that you're not alone Alex, and whoever these people were that captured you, they might still have others. If we can figure out what exactly happened that night, we might be able to track them down and unravel this whole mystery."

Alex nodded. It was likely still a lot for him to take in. Ben's mind whirred with thoughts. He cast his gaze towards the city and the towering skyscraper that housed the offices of Cyan Enterprises. What mysteries did it hold? What did they want with Alex? It was foreboding and grim, and the other question that Ben was too afraid to ask was why had they had let him go? Why give him to Hammond? It was likely that whatever they wanted from Alex they had gotten, but what was it exactly?

Ben stayed there and held him for a while.

"What do we do now?" Alex asked.

"We'll keep digging. Maybe there are other memories locked inside your head. The only thing I'm worried about is piecing together Cyan's plan. It's not going to be easy to figure out what they were doing, and I doubt they're going to have publicized a raid on a pack of werewolves. I'm afraid there's only one man who knows their agenda."

"Hammond," Alex said.

Ben nodded soberly. "I know you don't want to go back to him. Part of me wants to tell you to stay with me and ignore him completely, to leave that life behind. I don't like the idea of you being around him because if he suspects anything..." Ben trailed off, unable to speak the unthinkable.

"But it might be the only way to know the truth. I have to go back to him. I have to fight if he needs me to fight, until I can get him to tell me the truth."

"I wish there was another way," Ben said helplessly.

"No, it's okay. This time I know I'll be fighting for something. This time I go back there knowing something that he doesn't know. I know myself, and I know what I must do. It's going to be easier." There was a strength and confidence in Alex's voice that had been absent before. He blinked back his tears. His sorrow was replaced with an ice cold determination. He rose and pressed his lips together.

"Thank you, Ben. Thank you for everything."

"Thank *you, Alex*. You know that this is just the beginning, right?" Ben took Alex's hand. Alex smiled and nodded. Then, he tilted his head forward and kissed Alex, softly and sweetly.

"I know, we'll see each other again soon. There is something I have to do before I return to Mr. Hammond. For one night I want to know what life should be like for me, the life that my mother intended for me. For one night I want to be a wolf."

Ben nodded. They kissed again, and then Alex walked away, shifting into a wolf. Ben was astounded at the sight of the beast where the man had once been. He was filled with a sense of pride that he was able to witness something secret and magical. The heat of the kiss lingered on his lips and he knew that this was more than just a story. This was a crusade for a man's soul, the man that he was falling in love with.

Ben heard a howl in the distance, and then he smiled and returned home. When he got into his apartment he sat on the couch and pressed his hand against the fabric, remembering the electric lovemaking that he had experienced. The touch of Alex's flesh against his made him twitch with delight and he longed for the moment when he could be intimate with Alex again. Ben dragged himself to bed and sighed with happiness as he pulled the covers around him and wrapped his arms around him tightly, mimicking the warmth that came with being close to Alex.

He thought about his own past and how he had struggled with his place in the world and what he truly meant to people. If he could help Alex find the truth to his story and even reunite with his estranged mother, it might help Ben sleep better at night. He hadn't been entirely truthful with Alex. There was still one thing that tormented Ben; the way he had treated his biological mother. He had been so consumed with bitterness and hatred that he hadn't been kind to her at all and he hadn't given her what she was looking for. But had he denied himself something as well? Was he missing out on something that she could teach him? Perhaps there was still something missing, just like there was something missing from Alex. His mother had been the key. Perhaps Ben's mother was the key as well.

Either way, it didn't matter. He had bigger things to worry about now. The thought of uncovering something that the Cyan company wanted to keep secret was going to be challenging, and Cyan was far more dangerous than Hammond. Ben just hoped they weren't biting off more than they could chew, and he hoped more than anything that Alex would stay safe.

Chapter Thirteen

The night was more alive than Alex had ever known it. The scents on the air were powerful and the horizon burst with possibilities. His wolf mind was keen and he tasted so many different things. As he looked at the moon he howled, but this time it was not a howl of mourning, but a howl of a triumph. It was a howl made for all the wolves out there, to anyone who was listening, declaring that he had discovered a sacred part of himself and he wasn't going to ignore it again. He was out and he would use his knowledge to help those in need.

In the shadows of the night he knew he could run away and leave this all behind. There may still have been some kind of mystery about himself, but he knew enough that he wasn't the type of person to leave situations like this. His feelings for Ben were powerful, but more than that, there were others who needed him. If there was a chance of finding his mother then he wanted to take it, no matter how dark the path was.

He raced through the city, keeping to the shadows and back alleys so that nobody saw him. He ran until his lungs were bursting. He pushed himself to his limits and he felt stronger than he had ever been before. Then, he skulked back towards Mr. Hammond's bar, filled with a new feeling in his heart. This time he wasn't so uncertain or afraid. He knew what his purpose was in the world and he wasn't going to let anyone else tell him otherwise, not even Mr. Hammond. Before he got within the vicinity of Mr. Hammond's bar, he shifted back into a man and focused on what he had to do. It wasn't going to be easy to get information from Mr. Hammond, so he would have to take his time and ensure that he was beyond reproach. It was going to be a long, arduous process and he was going to have to do things he didn't want to do, but at least by the end of it he would have answers, and if Mr. Hammond had anything to do with harming his mother, Alex would make him pay.

***

When Alex returned, the bar was bustling with energy. Men had smiles on their faces and the girls were laughing happily, creating the illusion that it was the most magical night of their lives. As Alex gazed upon it, he looked at it with disgust, knowing that Mr. Hammond peddled nothing but lies. Now that he had experienced something real with Alex, he knew how hollow this place truly was. He hadn't been able to see it before because he hadn't known any better, but now it was plain to see, and it made his stomach turn.

"Oh, you're back," Andrea slurred. Mr. Hammond's wife was sitting at the bar, leaning on the counter. Her eyes were glassy and her face was etched into a scowl. Ruby lipstick was smeared across her lips and she looked tired. The usual high energy was absent, and this time her eyes did not sparkle as brightly as her jewelry. There were a number of empty glasses beside her, and one that was half filled.

"Richie has been looking for you. It makes me sick. I wish he'd be that upset at me if I ran away," she spat his name and spoke with a dry laugh. "He wants to see you in his office. You should know better than to leave."

"I just wanted to take a break from this place. And I'm sure he'd miss you," Alex replied. Andrea snorted and sipped at her drink.

"That's what I love about you Alex, you have no idea what's really going on here," she sighed and placed her hand against his arm, squeezing it gently. "You should know better than to leave him for this long. It was a lesson I learned a long time ago."

"Why? I'm not a prisoner," Alex said indignantly.

Andrea threw her head back and laughed. "Darling, we're all prisoners one way or another." She raised her hand and wiggled her fingers at him. The jewelry danced as it caught the light. There was no humor in her eyes, and Alex found himself feeling sorry for her. Perhaps she had always been like this and he simply hadn't been able to see it before. "Anyway, you shouldn't go and keep the master waiting. He's already angry enough," she gestured with a wave of the hand towards Mr. Hammond's office, and then turned back to her drink. She finished off what remained in her glass and then tapped the bar, gesturing for the bartender to pour her another. Alex left her to go and face Mr. Hammond.

***

As he walked towards the office he glanced around the bar and pondered Andrea's words. He knew many of the girls here, but he had never looked at them particularly closely. Now that he did, he saw that just after they laughed, they turned their heads away and the expression fell into something dark and grim. It was all an act, and it was like they were prisoners. Perhaps he could do something to help them.

He took a deep breath before he entered the office, knowing that Mr. Hammond would be angry. He opened the door. Mr. Hammond was waiting there, perusing some files. He glanced up.

"Take a seat Alex," he said. His voice was as cold as stone. As soon as Alex sat down Mr. Hammond stood up and walked around behind him.

"You should know better than to leave this place without telling me. You're very valuable to me. I don't appreciate you leaving for this long. Where were you?" Alex squirmed in his chair, noticing the undercurrent of anger that simmered in his voice.

"Just walking. I had to go and think."

"*Walking*? Thinking?" Mr. Hammond spat. "You're not here to walk and think. You're here to fight. This is about what you've been talking about, isn't it? This is about you developing a conscience, like some little girl. Let me tell you something Alex. If you want to be anything in this world then you need to be ruthless. You can't have room for a conscience. Do you think I got to where I am today because I cared about people? Do you think I built my little empire on promises and favors and charity? No, because to be successful you can't have room for that. It cost me a lot along the way, I can tell you that, but it's all worth it, and it's the same for you. I didn't bring you here to care. I brought you to fight. It's what you're good at. It's what you're good for. The arena is where you belong and it's the only thing that should matter. Now I don't care what you're thinking about. The people you fight aren't good people, but you'll fight whoever I tell you to fight, even if I told you to fight the Pope. This is your job. It's what I have you here. I own the thing inside you. I've trained you and I'm not going to let something like a conscience get in the way. You think that beast inside you cares? It doesn't have a conscience." He leaned over the back of Alex's chair, curling his hands over the back. His breath was hot and full of fury, and spittle flew from his mouth. The next words were filled with a grim threat.

"Do I need to take you to the chains again? I thought you had learned all the lessons I had to teach you, but perhaps I was wrong? Maybe you need to learn again. I'll lash you within an inch of your life if I have to boy, as long as you learn your place in this world. I have you and I will make use of you the way I see fit. You will fight for me and you will be happy to do it, and by the end of it we will both be very rich men. Is that understood? I don't have any time for you to think or to have feelings about this. You're a beast, nothing more and nothing less. Now go back to your room and wait there until I have a need for you, and don't you dare think about leaving without permission again."

"Yes Mr. Hammond," Alex said with a wavering voice. He rose and walked out of the office with his head held high, holding his tongue because for the first time he was actually filled with the courage to fight back. When Mr. Hammond had treated him like this before, Alex had always been filled with fear, but no longer. Now he knew that Mr. Hammond had no power over him. Alex was only here because he had chosen to stay, not because Mr. Hammond had decided it. He would only fight until he knew the truth, and then he would have another conversation with Mr. Hammond, but this time *he* would be the one dictating the terms.

***

Alex returned to his room and his heart sank as he looked at the small place he called his own. Here there was no Ben, and no reminders of his actual life. He thought about the future and the fights that he might have to endure. Mr. Hammond might have called him just a beast, but Alex knew he was more than that. The beast inside him wasn't a mask, it was just another side of his personality, one that he still had to learn a lot about. Mr. Hammond might have thought of him as just a mindless monster, but Alex knew that wasn't the case. For the first time in a long time he knew more than Mr. Hammond, and he knew himself.

He thought about his mother's words. He was somebody's son, a child of the moon. He meant a lot to Ben as well. For the first time his heart was being filled with emotions other than longing and anguish and pain. He wasn't consumed by anger and blood lust. The only fight left was one from the truth, and now he had an ally. He closed his eyes and thought back. It was still difficult him to work through the darkness and find new memories, but at least he had the new memories to think about and the image of his mother's face. No longer did he have to look at shadows when he looked back in his mind, but he could see a face that stared at him with love. Her eyes were kind and beautiful, and he felt safe when he thought of her.

She had been right when she said that this world was dangerous, and Mr. Hammond was part of the danger. Whoever had captured them was part of the danger as well, but Alex would find them, no matter what. He didn't care what Mr. Hammond said either, there was no way he was going to be a prisoner here. He would leave when he wanted to as nothing was going to stop him from seeing Ben again. He had another fight to fight, one that was more difficult than any other, but at least this fight was a way to regain his soul, not to lose it.

He rose from the bed and walked to the window. The moon hung high in the sky. Alex had always been drawn to it, even when he remembered nothing else there was still this connection to the moon. He had remembered much already, but this gave him a feeling that the rest would return at some point, and that it was still inside him, just waiting for him to remember. A smile played upon his lips as he basked in the silver glow of the moon.

"I'm coming for you Mom, wherever you are. I promise that I will find you."

9 7 9 8 7 1 8 9 6 1 4 6 1